WHISKEY SIX

Roy Sinclair

To Wendy
Love,
Betty

Trafford
PUBLISHING™

www.trafford.com

North America & international
toll-free: 1 888 232 4444 (USA & Canada)
phone: 250 383 6864 ♦ fax: 250 383 6804
email: info@trafford.com

The United Kingdom & Europe
phone: +44 (0)1865 722 113 ♦ local rate: 0845 230 9601
facsimile: +44 (0)1865 722 868 ♦ email: info.uk@trafford.com

10 9 8 7 6 5 4 3

Introduction

The man who dug the ditch was not named Ruff. Nor was the small prairie on which he settled nor the lake one ridge over from his house. But the ditch is there and can still be found. So can the last rotting remnants of his flume and the wooden pipeline leading to it if you know where to look.

'Ed's' log house still stands on it's hillside bench near the Kootenay River but the roof has fallen in.

The Spreading Pine is patterned on a real sawmill with a small settlement for employees to live close to their work. The present day Dorr Cutoff Road which leaves Highway 93 about three kilometres south of the new Elk River Bridge passes smack through the middle of what used to be the log pond and goes full length of where the sawmill building once stood. All the characters who lived there for this story are fictitious—the story itself is not a true one. Much licence has been taken with time and sequence of events.

The old Elk Canyon grade as described was real and awesome by today's highway standards. It was always closed at the first snowfall in autumn and not used again until bare and dry in springtime. Depending on your tires even a rainstorm could be bad news. If you lived south of the Elk River prior to the mid

1950's it left you feeling tied to Montana for the winter though there was another, longer, occasionally snowplowed way out to the rest of British Columbia.

The Canadian Army blew up the bridge a few years ago for demolition practice.

Whiskey Six—the cast

Eddy
A nineteen year old, half Indian, cowboy kid who owns a good horse and a bad rifle. A natural mechanical genius with uneducated engineering skills he is always willing and eager to help anyone in need—from Lawman to lawbreaker.

Buck
Eddy's horse—once belonged to a bandit known to have been a killer from ambush. The bandit happens to have been Eddy's now deceased father.

Ruff
A dryland homesteader in his forties—one of those unfortunate people who can never do anything right. His rifle is a good one but he has no horse and is too honest for his own good.

Amy
Ruff's eighteen year old daughter—she has one boyfriend too many and a true gamblers instinct.

Libby
Ruff's first wife and Amy's mother. Always an optimist she sent Amy into exile on Ruff's home-

stead to separate her from an undesirable element. She is coming on the train.

Corrie	Ruff's playful, second and already separated present wife just four years older than Amy. She cooks at Mr. Simon's sawmill camp.
Reece	The undesirable element but not so much a gangster as his father was. He is coming by car faster than the train.
Reb	Eddy's mother—soft spoken 'Dr. without letters.'
Hettie	Eddy's sister—a girl prettier than she wants to be.
Percy	Hettie's—um—husband. A very lucky man.
Mr. Simon	Owner of the sawmill—with this Depression thing coming on and Eddy maintaining his car he has plenty to worry about.
Errol	Eldest of the Fuller brothers—he is Mr. Simon's Time Keeper and righthand man in the office. Eddy see's him as Coyote—opportunist- not to be trusted around any henhouse.
Floyd	Errol's younger brother. He is the flunky who works with Corrie but it's his brother who plays with her. The Brothers Fuller would like to be Ranchers.

Chapter One

Sure footed little Buck was falling—going down so sudden that his rider had no time to swing clear. The ground was coming up fast and he knew it was going to hurt.

In the tiny loft of the saddle and harness shed where he slept, nineteen year old Ed Cameron sat up with a jerk that sent a tremor all through the upper reaches of the small frame building. It was dark yet—totally dark.

"A dream," he breathed in relief, "nothing but a dream." Still, he rubbed his left cheek where it seemed to smart from contact with the ground but there was no feel of blood or injury so he stretched out once more hoping to sleep until dawn.

Hot! Too hot for May.

But that's May for you, 80 in the shade like today or blowing a blizzard across the mountain faces tomorrow. The slight and fickle movement of air from the south offered no relief other than to stay in the shade but for those who had to work in the open there was little chance of that.

Like the man working alternately with grub hoe or shovel digging a ditch along a slope of ground at the south end of the lumber yard.

Two others who also had no choice were piling boards to air dry before being planed and sold. The 'plop' of each board dropping was steady as the beat of music until one struck 'off tune' as if the wrong string had been plucked. A pause then while the errant board was kicked into place before the beat continued.

Faint as the breeze was it brought the scent of lustful springtime excesses from overheated sage brush, pine and fir in cloying waves adding a fragrant stuffiness to the afternoon. It did help though to carry the 'buzz—zzaw' and rumble noises of the sawmill away to the north. The 'chow—- pow' exhaust of the 'shotgun' steam feed of the carriage was not so easily muted and came from it's tall stack persistent as a one gun artillery barrage.

Only the horse and rider, easing along southward through the shade of one big pine and on to the next while following no particular path, seemed unaffected by the heat. They circled around the lumber yard and came upon the ditch digger as if by accident.

"Here now, what're you staring at?"

The voice might have been less gruff had the speaker been less startled to find himself watched by, not one but two pairs of eyes—those of the horse as well as the rider. The rider's eyes were sleepy lidded but the horse stared openly with curiosity and humour as if the animal were ready to burst into laughter at the slightest provocation. He hadn't heard them approach.

"Never seen water run uphill."

"Now that's a fool thing to say 'cause you likely never will."

"Too bad."

The man shuffled his feet and changed his stance to face his visitor more squarely then automatically set one foot on the shovel blade and leaned a little on the handle.

"What's that supposed to mean, Indian Kid?"

The kid pulled his right foot from the stirrup and shifted about till his knee was hooked around the horn of his slick forked saddle. Both feet were now on the same side of the horse.

Somehow the horse took on a more restful pose too.

"Not Indian."

"Eh, sorry, didn't mean to hurt your tender feelings."

The kid's eyes became even sleepier.

"Feelings not tender. Not hurt either. Just don't qualify."

"Well, you look kind of Indian."

He looked the other over more closely then—wide brimmed black hat with coins and badges sewn to it and long black hair showing most of the way around. His shirt was definitely intended to say 'cowboy'. So too was the wide leather belt cinched tight to hold up the pants that were far too loose for his skinny frame. Shiny brass rifle cartridges filled about half of the belt loops their weight adding to the necessary tightness of the belt. His high heeled riding boots were old and scuffed but clean and well oiled the spurs on them being the only part of the picture that might be new and maybe expensive. The attitude of the horse said they were unused and unnecessary—cosmetic only.

The horse too was a mix of old and new—neat little buckskin with a black stripe from mane to tail, a white star on his forehead and white stockings at all four feet. The obviously very old saddle had a flat topped horn big enough to lay a sandwich on and like the boots, showed a lot of wear but also a lot of recent care—it creaked at every move of horse or rider. The new looking bridle was probably meant to pass for a work of art but cheap machine tooling and imitation silver trim spilled the beans. 'Best if Amy never gets a look at this pair,' the ditch digger thought, 'she'd be head over heels after one glance.'

"And you look kind of hot and bothered," the kid said.

"Yes, and so I am. Why don't you get on your way and I'll be less bothered at least."

Without a word the kid did just that with one knee still hooked around the saddle horn—the little buckskin smooth gaited and sure footed.

❀❀❀

"Huh! You again." He hoped his little jump of surprise hadn't been as obvious to the kid as it had felt to him for once more he hadn't heard the horse approaching. They were simply there when he happened to look up—the horse with ears forward and eyes curious but the kid just watching with little interest. It came across almost as insolence.

"Get out of here you stupid kid who is not Indian and leave me alone."

The horse swung away, keen to travel whether the rider was or not.

"Wait a minute."

Once more with no apparent command the little buckskin, eyes bright with interest, walked a tight half circle returning to the man with the shovel.

"What'd you mean by that dumb remark yesterday about water running uphill?"

"Well. It's got to doesn't it? I mean if it's going to get out of this gully you seem intent on leading it into."

"You're crazy."

"That's possible. Been accused of it before."

"It's downhill all the way through to the road where I have the culvert ready and waiting for it."

"Okay." Horse and rider turned away and this time the ditch digger let them go.

❀ ❀ ❀

"Well smart alec kid who is not an Indian—you knew it all along didn't you."

"Aw. Not for sure. But it did look uphill to me. Too bad you didn't have the water following you every day then you'd not have done so much work for nothing. You'd have seen it wouldn't go."

"Well, I couldn't! The log pond was filling so none ran out into my ditch until today."

"How come did you let them take over your ditch from old Chrysler's to where they built the mill? You had a little water spilling down the hill four or five years ago and now you're only a quarter of a mile farther along and right up a gully."

The ditch digger looked at the kid in exasperated silence for a moment before answering. "If you know all that then you should've noticed it was only in the spring during high water that I got it to come all the way. I was losing too much across those gravel patches where it was sinking."

"You never tried walking horses through the water in your ditch—that might have helped."

"How?"

"Well. Reckon I wouldn't know much about it would I? But I've heard it said that Edward Charlie did that and got water out to the end of his ditch. The horses stir up the mud and that helps seal the leaks. Reckon his ditch was almost as long as yours."

"But he still gave up and left didn't he?"

"I reckon so. Just like all the other drylanders have done—except for you—you're the last one still trying. Lots of empty houses out there now."

They stared at each other—the strongly built man in his forties and the gangling kid in his oversize jeans.

"This one'll not be quitting."

"Okay."

"I can get it through this. I just need to back up to the corner there where it's sinking and dig it a little deeper to increase the grade."

"What for? To give it a run at the hill?"

The ditch digger now seemed to deny what he had more or less admitted only a moment ago, "I won't have to go down much to get it to the road."

The kid swung off his horse and stood beside the ditch looking one way and then the other.

"Only about five feet—up—not down—to get out the head of this gully and join up there at the road."

"You're crazy!"

"Aw. I guess you better hope so."

The kid swung back onto his horse. "See you again tomorrow."

❁ ❁ ❁

"Back again?"

"Sure. And I walked my horse down your ditch in the water. Might help."

"So now I can't drink from the ditch!"

"Hey! Was I you I wouldn't drink from that thing in the best of times. With log pond, cows, horses and kids along the way I don't think me and Buck can hurt it much."

"Yes, I know, you just surprise me, I thought you didn't care if it worked or not. I've got my canvas bag here for drinking water—I fill it at the pipe every morning and a fellow at the mill who has a truck hauls a couple of barrels from there to the house every Sunday."

"That ain't so great either after it comes under old Chrysler's outhouse and through his barnyard."

"Should be okay again after coming so far."

"Aw. I dunno. I sure wouldn't take the chance—not with it shut up in a pipe most of the way where it don't get no sunshine or air."

"Everyone at the mill camp uses it."

"Yeah. They do. They boil it first too."

"Oh. I didn't know that."

Neither said anything for a moment while the man wondered if this kid really knew what he talked about or just made it up as he went.

"You know? I will always wonder why you let them put it in that pipe 'cause you lost control of it as soon as that was done and the mill was built here. Only good thing is it's a wooden pipe and not iron."

"Don't like iron pipe?"

"Not for such a long ways—not healthy stuff—all rust and Lord knows what. Must be in that pipe for over a mile."

"It is and you are right about losing control but you don't understand at all. It had me beat. Actually I'd already given up hope of ever getting water this far when Simon came along and offered to put it in a pipe if he could use my ditch to lay it in. Now I can have the runoff from the log pond in return and that's at least something while the way it was working out till then it looked like I was going to wind up with nothing."

"If that there pond keeps leaking and evaporating the way it has so far you might not have so much anyway."

"I've seen these log ponds before and after a little while, with all the mud and bark that builds up on the bottom, they pretty soon quit leaking completely. This one is pretty much sealed now and I'm probably getting every drop that pipe brings to the mill."

"Only now you got to make it climb this hill."

"I'll get it through."

"Okay. But. I'm gonna tell Amy to boil the water you bring to her. Don't imagine she knows enough to do that if you didn't."

The ditch digger's hand slipped off the shovel handle and the weight of his foot on the blade drove it away from him—it clattered on the rocky bottom of the trench.

"Now wait a minute! How d'you happen to know my daughter's name?"

"Well. She didn't make no secret of it. Why shouldn't I know?"

Amy's father could think of several reasons beginning with, 'I thought she was alone all day. She hasn't said anything about being introduced to you—or to anyone else either for that matter,' but he didn't say it out loud. It's why she was here for the summer and maybe longer if the right sort of young man could be found to catch her interest. Her mother—his ex-wife of years ago—had sent her to him in a desperate effort to separate her from the "undesirable element" she had taken up with at their present home. He sure as the devil wasn't going to allow anything to develop between her and this too good looking and sassy kid. At least he had enough sense to refrain from blustering threats and orders to stay away even though he wanted to.

"I still think you look Indian. How come d'you say you're not?"

"Aw. What I said was, 'I don't qualify.'"

"What does that mean?"

"Well. I reckon some of my ancestors were Indian but various levels of white blood have been lifting the back edge of the tepee off and on ever since. So now about the very best I can claim to be is somewhere around halfbreed."

"I always thought the word 'halfbreed' was an insult but you don't seem to mind using it."

"Aw. Maybe it is an insult if you ain't one but I don't see any way it can be if you are. Pretty good state of affairs actually. Allows me to be whichever suits my notion of the day."

"Hm. I'm from the Old Country myself and it doesn't bother me to be called an Englishman even if some who say it don't mean it as a compliment so I guess I see your point."

14

"You know? I'd say you are even less an Englishman than I am an Indian. Don't see no signs hung out on you."

"Some never notice while others pick it up right away. Got all my schooling over here but there must still be a few—'signs hung out'—as you say. But don't you bother going around by my place to tell Amy about the water—I'll tell her myself when I get home which will be pretty soon now. I just want to bring that stream along to about here for today." He glanced back fifty feet to where the last of the water was sinking into the ground without having advanced one inch since the sun had warmed up the day.

"Oh. No sweat there. I'm going by anyhow for tea and cake with her so it's not out of my way. But I thought you knew enough to get your house water from over by the mountains. I ain't too keen on eating nor drinking much more at your place now that I found out different." The kid kneed Buck around and set off at the run to make up for lost time.

The ditch digger held a hand up—mouthed a few words—too little too late. Shouted as loud as he could—still too late—bent down for the fallen shovel and in a fit of frustration threw it as hard as he could after the kid who was already far beyond the reach of anything slower than a rifle bullet. But his aim was bad—the shovel caught in the limbs of a young fir tree—they bent then rebounded sending the shovel back nearly to his feet. He stared at it—almost willing to laugh at himself but refusing to do so for to laugh, he feared, might be admitting the kid was right. Or worse yet—it might be rueful admittance that he still had a temper after all—it was many years since he had resorted to throwing something. 'Darned kid and his highfalutin' ways— you'd think he was royalty and I was just a—a ditch digger.'

And then he did grin but it was thoughts of Libby being presented with a half Indian, cowboy son-in-law in loose britches that brought it on. His grin widened at thought of the loose britches—. 'It would be my fault, of course, for not getting her out sooner to meet the 'right' people here. But it's only been two weeks and I've been so busy. Didn't take the kid long to find her! Worse could happen I guess—she could've kept on with that "up and coming gangster," to quote Libby's words that she was getting mixed up with out at the Coast.'

Whatever might or might not be growing between Amy and the kid was evidently already underway. No use getting excited now—just have to find a way to derail it without appearing to have done so. He picked up the shovel and walked to where the last of the water was sinking but he didn't even wet the blade, instead, he looked one way along his ditch and then the other as the kid had done. The double slope of ground here might be creating an optical illusion. "I should've had this part surveyed too."

"Stupid, know-it-all kid. He might be right!"

Chapter 2

The ditch digger tossed his shovel behind the same bush that hid his grubhoe, pick and axe then struck off walking but not toward home. Home was two miles away to the south—by the time he got there he would be third one in on a party for two—a gate crasher in his own home. His own youth seemed a long time ago now but he could remember it well enough and still relate to it. Libby had been eighteen when they were married—the same age Amy is now. If he roared in objecting to her visitor she would latch on to the kid just to be ornery. Just as Libby had done. "Take it casual, my boy, take it casual."

But now he understood the boy's chip on the shoulder behaviour—'accept me or see if you can run me off'—he didn't know that Amy was keeping him a secret. "Right about now he is probably as confused as I am."

So he walked northward to the sawmill camp—to what posed as store and post office where mail was picked up and delivered three days a week by car borne connection with the CPR passenger train. It bore the name of 'Flagstone' which was not the name of this place at all. In fact, this place had no name and no one even lived here until Simon piped in the water and built his

Spreading Pine Lumber operation. A few families followed for the work and then the post office—needing customers—came too.

"Flagstone" was actually the name of the town miles away beside the Kootenay River where the post office had been until the sawmill there closed down and everyone moved away. Easier to skid the shack that carried the name than to change it. This sawmill too will only last until the close timber is gone and then no doubt "Flagstone" will be trundled off somewhere else. As long as the driver of the mail car knows where it goes—those in Ottawa need not.

The only mail today was his copy of a weekly newspaper and two letters, both addressed in Libby's bold style, a thick and heavy one for Amy and a very light one for him—her usual one pager no doubt. He put both in a shirt pocket—went to the store counter and bought two chocolate bars to take home. Then he remembered—considered—dug deeper to buy a third and dropped it into the paper bag with the other two.

Half way home he pulled his own letter from his pocket and dropped it inside his shirt out of sight. Amy might ask questions if she saw it. He wasn't sure yet he would even bother to open and read it since Libby seldom had anything nice to say by letter. She had not remarried and though it was well after their divorce before he did, she had taken it very badly. Since then her letters had been masterpieces of sarcasm and their daughter had no longer been allowed to spend the summers with him on what was becoming known locally as Ruff's Prairie, or lately, as Ruff's Folly. Even so it hadn't surprised him that she turned to him for help when she wanted "a quiet place out in the country where people are honest and law abiding." A place to send Amy in hopes of her finding a safer romance. What did surprise him was that Amy hadn't objected other than being a bit huffy the first few days here. Perhaps the kid was the reason her outlook had improved.

At home, other than horse tracks in the yard, there was no sign of the kid but there were two cups and two desert plates in the sink—very careless of her. He made a mental note to hide the chocolate bars until some other time—they would be too melted to unwrap now anyway.

"What's this, Amy? Both your breakfast and lunch dishes not washed yet?"

She didn't even blink an eye. "With the water having to be hauled and in such short supply it's not worth washing just a few. I left them to do with our supper things."

'Well, she didn't lie about it—she just failed to tell the truth.'

As the meal progressed with a free flow of sometimes interesting small talk between them, Ruff even began to wonder if the kid had really been here—until—.

"Father," with her nose in her water glass, "this stuff doesn't smell very good. Are you sure it's safe to drink without boiling?"

He was here alright! Shifty little lady. Takes after her mother.

"If it'll make you feel better then by all means boil it. Sure won't hurt anything and it might keep us from getting sick. Glad you thought of it."

After the meal and the cleanup was all taken care of and he was settling down with the newspaper she came from her room dressed in jeans and shirt, walking shoes and a straw hat. She looked like she belonged here and that both pleased and worried him. He liked seeing her acting 'at home' in the country but thinking of the kid, he worried now just how thoroughly she planned to become a part of it.

"I'm going for a walk along the ridge, Dad. I'll be back before dark."

'I should hope so,' he thought, 'dark is four hours away yet.' "Which ridge?"

She pointed east, back of the house and away from the road. He went to the window and watched her go. So like her mother—medium tall—dark brown hair worn long—takes a tan well. So well that right now she is nearly as dark skinned as the kid. He watched her out of sight as she went more to the south than to the east where she had pointed.

The Reservation is that way. If that's where the kid lives then that's the way he would come from to meet her. But today he came openly and served notice that he was doing so—he wouldn't come again clandestinely would he? Who else could she be meeting? No one of course! She's only been here for two weeks and pretty well confined to the house at that. She grew up here until she was twelve and then spent her summers here until three years ago so she might have a friend within walking distance. That is—if they both walked toward a common goal halfway between and didn't spend a lot of time visiting before returning to their respective homes.

The kid on his horse could come any distance.

'I could follow but if she see's me that's worse than sitting here wondering—quite unforgivable—she is eighteen after all. I have to assume it's just as she says and she is out for no more than a walk.' He tried to get interested in the squabbles racking the Fernie City Council but found it impossible and soon put the paper down. In fact, he decided, he was in a perfect mood to tackle Libby's letter. Pulling it from inside his shirt he was about to rip it open when he caught up to himself and reached for the letter opener instead to do it in his usual neat fashion

His eyes flew to the salutation wondering if he had graduated yet to Dear Truman or Dear Mr. Ruff or for that matter—dear anything warmer than the plain and stark 'Ruff' that she had used the last three years.

Only there wasn't one! Nothing! She just went straight into her message. He scanned down the page and found it, as usual, short and sweet—well—it was short—sweet was yet to be proven. And there was no signature. He turned it over but the other side was blank. Back to the front and this time he read it.

I don't know what we are getting into but that wannabe Mafia mobster knocked on my door this morning and waved a letter from Amy under my nose. He held it so I could read some of it but not reach it. So help me, it was practically a love letter! But that's beside the point—what you need to know is she told him where she is and even drew a map of ~~ou~~ your farm and all the roads leading to it. <u>And she heavy, dark lined the back road coming in from the sharp corner on the Dorr road just north of Edwards Lake! She obviously takes after your sister Edith!</u>

He said he is busy right now but as soon as he has time he is going for her. He carries a gun! His jacket was open enough that I could see the shoulder harness to hold it. He told me to stand back and stay out of his and Amy's affair (that's the word he used) then he laughed at me! He scared me very badly. I tremble yet just writing this and thinking about him.

There is only one way to deal with this. If you love your daughter—shoot him—give him no chance because he will give you none. Bury him deep and take his car apart and bury the pieces. He drives a black McLaughlin Super Six. If you see a car like you have never seen before—that's him.

He is still here today so you have a little time yet to plan. I'll write again as soon as I think he has left town. Burn this! Right now!"

Ruff read it again slower and quite calmly. He had not yet decided if he should laugh at Libby's hysteria or be shocked out of his skin by her suggested solution to the matter.

Amy had walked in a direction that would soon see her on the road she had dark lined on her map! But he won't be here yet—unless—he grabbed the envelope and looked for the stamp cancellation. Posted day before yesterday so it made a good connection between the train and local delivery. No, he won't be here yet unless he was already on his way as Libby was writing this warning despite having told her he was busy.

A gangster! How unlikely. Amy is far too sensible for that. Too sensible to fall for the kid too. It's just that he is handy and so different than anyone she's ever run into before. Perhaps it's natural she would find him interesting in a trivial way for a while. 'I think Libby's trolley has gotten off the track and time will show her that.' He went to the stove and burned both letter and envelope.

He had enough of his own problems without this and getting water to this dry piece of real estate might not be the biggest of them. His present wife, Corrie, might take that honour. She worked at the Spreading Pine cookhouse feeding the men who lived in the bunkhouses and worked in the mill or out in the woods. Her wages were their only income while he tried to get water to this dry place to transform it to the truck garden business that he dreamed of. Horses and cattle or livestock of any description held no appeal for Ruff. He wanted to grow vegetables and perhaps even flowers and shrubs for decorative purposes though he knew there would be precious little market for such frivolities for some years yet. Not until the nearby towns grew bigger but that was where his thoughts and hopes lay.

Corrie was younger than Libby which sat well with her but not with Libby. The two had met but it could not be described as amicable by even the remotest stretch of the imagination. Amy had not been present nor had she ever met her stepmother despite now living in the home that was Corrie's.

All last winter, Ruff, sometimes addressed as Tru but almost never as Truman, and Corrie, lived in the cook's quarters at the camp and he worked in the mill. Once the road dried up in springtime they moved back home to the farm two miles south of the mill and Ruff quit his job to return to making the farm and ditch into something workable. Everything he wanted in this life hinged on getting water to his fields. He was sure he could endure almost any hardship or indignity even such as living on his wife's income as long as it helped get him to his long term goal of being a full time professional gardener.

After they moved back home he drove Corrie to work early every morning in the old Studebaker that right now sat out back with a nearly dry gasoline tank. He had picked her up again in the evening to bring her home. It made a long day for her but there were a couple of hours of free time both morning and afternoon when she could rest or even sleep in her private room within the cookhouse building.

With the sudden arrival of Amy, announced with just enough advance warning for Corrie to pack, she served notice that she would not share the house with "that brat of a kid of yours". She was four years older than Amy.

"But, Cor, I think she is finished with school so I doubt she will be going back to that. She might be with us for a long time—maybe until she gets married."

"Then I am up there for a long time or until she gets married," and she pointed north to the Spreading Pine. "And don't bring her to visit! It might be best if you don't come either."

In a way it was just as well because the Studebaker was giving up the ghost. It would still come from the mill in high gear but had to be shifted down to pull the ever so slight grade going northward. A grade it hadn't even noticed when it was running right. He had no idea what might be wrong and if someone had told him what it was then he had no mechanical skill to fix it anyway. There was no money to hire a mechanic or to buy parts and nothing to trade for help. If he had a close enough friend he might have been able to lean on that—except he wouldn't—always willing to help others if their need was brought to his attention nonetheless he shunned help from others.

'Maybe I had better take a walk too seeing as it's cooling down a little out there. Maybe I'll take the gun along and maybe I'll find myself on that road south of here accidentally. If I run into Amy it's not my fault since she said she was going to the hill.'

He had a good rifle—a 'two ridge gun'—and he was good with it. 'My green thumb and my trigger finger—they both know their business. Too bad I've never learned how to 'push a sharp pencil.' But if Libby thought he was going to shoot a man then she would have to think again because he could hardly bring himself to shoot a deer and seldom did so. Hadn't in years. About all he ever shot at now was a tin can on a fence post just to keep his hand and eye in practice.

'But I can play the role of the heavy fisted old hillbilly father with a long gun under my arm. That should scare off any city slicker who comes sneaking around.' He looked the part too with his ragged, nearly worn out clothes, long hair and eyes that seemed to glare even when he was in a good mood.

When he returned to the house hours later as darkness snaked it's long fingers through the valley tree by tree he found Amy at home preparing the gas lamp to read by.

"I was getting worried, father—I didn't know you were going out." She watched as he hung the rifle on the wall near the door.

"Just felt like I needed a walk too. What did your mother have to say?"

"Oh, nothing much, just the usual."

"About six pages to say the usual?"

"Oh well, you know mom, if there's a bush in sight she has to beat her way around it six times."

"Not with me she doesn't."

They both laughed.

Chapter 3

"Why d'you always show up at the same time each day and always coming from the north?" The little buckskin peered at him so intently that he wondered if he should have addressed the horse and not the rider.

"Well. I finish my work same time every day so now is when I'm free to be on my way."

"And what work is it that ends so soon after lunch each day? Sundays included 'cause you were here both weekend days. Seven days a week?"

"Right. Just like you. Every day. I split wood for the cookhouse stove there at the sawmill. The office and bunkhouses too only they aren't burning any in this weather."

"My wife is the cook there."

"I know."

So this is how he learned about Amy then. Corrie has her fine finger in this pie too. Aiming the kid southward and egging him on hoping for a match and an early wedding so she can be rid of his daughter. "It can't take long to split enough for the cook stove—you could have it done in the cool of the morning if you wanted—why so late all the time?"

For the first time since they had met, the kid smiled right up into his eyes. "That's easy. If I show up right at meal time and work on the woodpile as the crew eats then your wife feeds me when she and the flunky have their lunch. Since we are just eating from what's left over she don—doesn't make out a tab so I eat for free."

"Ah, I see. So now you are headed home. Why do I never see you on your way north to your job?" The kid was working so hard at keeping his grammar halfway proper that it was nearly comical after the way he had been mauling the English language earlier. 'He must think he has passed first muster with me so has dropped the chip that was on his shoulder. Now he is trying to impress upon me that he is not a totally uneducated dunce. But Amy has not yet said a word about him so he must be no more than amusement to fill in time until the main event gets here.' Ruff almost felt sorry for the boy and was suddenly drawn to look on him in a more friendly manner. Libby might too—as compared to her gangster type.

"Well. There's shorter ways. If I was headed home then you wouldn't see me now either. I go this way so I can stop by to visit with Amy." Then he smiled once more, "and get a second dessert. By the time I ride from here to there dinner is shook—shaken down and there's room for more." Then he changed the subject, "what do you plan to do now?" He nodded toward the ditch where the water still had not made it around the corner where it has been sinking ever since reaching that point.

"I've not decided yet. If I can get it to cross the road here I've got it made because that section from there all the way to the field was surveyed so I know it will work."

"You should have had this surveyed too."

"Surveyors don't work cheap but you are right, I should have had this end surveyed and done my guesswork below here. When it rains hard the water runs down the road in little rivers nearly to my place so there was never any doubt about that end having the right grade but I needed a marked line to follow as I dug the hillside part of it."

"Yeah. And from somewhere about here it also runs back toward the mill so you got high ground here."

"Yes, so it seems. I borrowed a level this morning and nailed a board to a tree then levelled it to sight along and I had to get it about four feet above the present water level to have any chance of crossing the road. And then I sighted back to the pond and it's just not going to happen from here. So I guess you were right." Just saying that—admitting it—cleared his mind of the mistake that was made and readied him to plan the necessary changes. Changes that he now realised, thanks to the kid's nagging, were already half formed in his mind. "They switch over from the wooden pipe at the top of the hill to the big iron pipe that brings it straight down to the pond. Then, just above the level of the truck road where they unload logs into the pond there are some fittings welded onto it."

"Yeah. I know where you mean. It's where they take off with the small pipe that goes to the boiler room and I reckon there must be a branch in it somewhere that goes to the cookhouse and probably Simon's house too."

"Yes, that's the place. If I start from there and ditch it along the hill behind the houses then I can flume it across the valley to this spot but high enough to get across to the road."

"Means you got to build a lot of flume." The kid looked across to the other hillside," must be all of two hundred feet at the very shortest spot you could do it."

"Got any better ideas?"

The kid and his horse both thought it over and Ruff half expected the answer to come from Buck but Buck held silence on the matter.

"Maybe. Once you have it on that hillside above the houses why not keep it there until you get over this rise in the valley floor and then start angling across to where you want it."

"No, I don't think so. I've got to get it to the west side of my field because that's the high side. Then I can flood irrigate down rows running eastward. Besides, there's all that work already done on this side including two culverts under the road."

"Well. You can still get to the high side farther down and you'll have more water to do it with so it might be worth abandoning some of your older work."

"Why would I have more water by going along the east side."

"Well. Looks to me like you wouldn't lose so much. There's good soil along that side instead of this gravel and stone you got out here. It wouldn't sink so much on you over there."

"What makes you think the soil is better on that side? Why would there be a difference one side to the other in such a narrow valley?"

"Aw. Reckon I wouldn't know why, would I? Unless it's because of what this valley used to be way back when the ice was melting. Reckon it was a river—a real big river—maybe so big once that it helped make this hundreds of miles long trench alongside the Rockies that we now call home. Who knows why a river dumps fine soil in one place and scours another down to stone and hardpan?"

"But, just from the middle of the valley here to that side, less than a hundred yards," Ruff looked where he had gestured, "there shouldn't be any difference."

"Seems not. But. I think there is.

"That's all very interesting but soil or no soil, the simple fact is I've got to get it to this side and meet up with what's already done and waiting as soon as I can. I don't want to get down there on the wrong side and find I can't get across to where I need it. I don't want any more mistakes like I made here so I will run grade with the level before I dig."

"You could do that on the east side too. At the very worst you might need a little flume there too to get across to where you want it but a lot less than here I reckon."

"No, I'll do my flume building here close to the lumber yard so I can buy boards from Simon when I need them. Then I can carry them over instead of having to hire someone to haul them as I would have to do if I were to build farther away."

"You could tie them on the side and haul them with your car."

"Well, the sad fact is, my car doesn't run and I don't know what's wrong with it."

"Oh. Amy didn't tell you?"

"Tell me what?"

"I fixed the car for you. It runs good now."

"How did you know it needed fixing?"

"Amy. Said she wanted you to take her to town but you told her the car wouldn't run so I checked it over then fixed it."

"What was wrong with it?"

"Oh. Not much. The spark plugs were pretty bad so I cleaned and gapped them but the main problem was the points. They were burned back right through the contact into the arm so I took them out and filed them flat but then I traded them for a better set and put the better ones in your car. The timing seemed a bit off too so I advanced the spark a mite."

"Huh!" Possibilities ran through Ruff's mind and he didn't like them at all. Where would the kid find a better set of points to 'trade for'? Who would trade for a set that was, by the sound of it, pretty much finished? Who else around here has a Studebaker?

'Oh no! It's a lot newer but some inside parts might be the same.'

"Tell me," (I've got to learn a name for this kid,) "is Simon having car trouble about now?"

"Aw. Not yet. He's okay for a few hundred miles and then, what the heck, he's got lots of money to buy new points. I've already told him he needs new ones." Seeing the question in Ruff's eyes he explained, "I do all his oil changes and keep his engine tuned up so I'll get you a set of newer spark plugs too—you need better ones."

"Uh, sure. Okay. Thanks." What else to say—at this late date?

"Look Kid, I've got to get to work, the afternoon is slipping by. If you waste much more time your tea will be cold and your cake dried out."

The kid grinned at him, "sure thing, see you tomorrow."

'I could hope otherwise,' Ruff thought. 'What will Simon say if he finds out?'

'If the kid is smiling at Amy like he smiled here then it's no wonder she is setting out tea and cake for him. And now I've gone and given him the impression that I approve of him calling on her—when she is alone at that! And on top of it all I have accepted stolen goods installed in my car!'

'I should go and tell Simon right now.'

Instead, he picked out the spot where the flume, yet to be built, must end in order to get water across to the road. There he nailed his board to a tree so he could use the level for sighting across to the other hillside. To be sure he was not making another mistake he packed his board and level across and sighted back to the spot where the flume must reach.

Once satisfied that he had allowed enough extra height on the hillside to meet his needs he repositioned the board and proceeded to mark out a ditch line toward the iron pipe where it came down the hill. 'The nice part about this,' he reflected, 'is that I don't have to come out to an exact spot since a short hose or pipe will put water in the beginning of the ditch no matter if it turns out to be above or below the fittings on the big pipe.

He had a few moments of doubt though when he realised his new line took him between the back doors of the short row of houses and their attendant outdoor biffies built along the hillside in a matching short row.

'Don't worry about it,' he advised himself, 'they should appreciate having water in their back yards. The kids certainly will.'

On his way home he did as the kid had more or less suggested and walked along the east side of the valley even though he had done so many times before and knew every inch of it. Certainly the soil had to be deep along here since the gopher mounds were all dirt and showed no rocks or gravel carried up from below. "Odd I've never noticed that before. It certainly would have been easier digging here." Some of the gopher holes were made larger by the workings of a badger and he guessed that must have meant tragedy for the smaller inhabitants.

At home he went straight to the car, turned on the ignition, carefully set the choke and throttle controls and got out the crank. The car had an electric self starter but he didn't want to drain the battery any lower than it already was after weeks of hard starting and more weeks of non use.

It started so easily that he just stood there with the crank in one hand staring at it in disbelief until it began choking itself. The smooth fast idle turned to a gallop with black smoke belching from the exhaust each time it raced up from a near stall. He made it to the driver's seat just in time to reset the choke to where it ran smoothly again. In a few more seconds he was able to move both choke and throttle to idle positions. The engine ticked along so quietly that he could hardly believe this was the same machine that had given him so much trouble getting home the last time he used it.

"That useless cowboy kid has wrought some kind of mechanical magic here."

He shut off the engine, slammed the car door as he exited and he slammed the house door too jerking Amy's attention up from her book.

Chapter 4

"So! Has he got a name?"

"What on earth are you talking about? Does who have a name?"

"That Indian kid who fixed the car so good that it runs like I have never heard it run before. That cowboy kid who comes here every day on his buckskin horse to drink our tea and eat our cake."

"Oh. You mean Eddy?"

"Yes! If that's his name then I mean Eddy."

"I should think you would be very happy that he has fixed the car. Now we can drive to town and do some proper shopping. We're getting awfully low on some things and your little store up the road seems very expensive and poorly stocked. I need some decent thread and darning wool too so I can mend your socks and I simply must find a fabric supply or you will be walking right out of your clothes. I have so much time on my hands when I could be doing so many useful things. And if you don't get out away from your work pretty soon you won't know how to talk to people—you can hardly put together a civil sentence now."

Just like her mother! She has turned the tables on him so that now he feels heavy handed and guilty for it. Still, he was boiling over inside and couldn't stop so quickly.

"Don't get interested in him Amy or you will find yourself living in a tepee, skinning out the deer he drags home and six kids underfoot within eight years."

"Father!"

He wheeled to go back outside before he could say worse.

"Don't go running off now, supper is ready. I just don't have it on the table but by the time you wash it will be."

Ashamed of himself, both for his outburst and now for his sudden meekness, he detoured to the washbasin where he spent twice his normal time cleaning up. He did feel better after splashing his face and hair with cool water. 'She's right, I've been working too hard but it's partly the heat too—mostly it's this hotter than normal weather getting to me. Or is it mostly that time consuming mistake that means starting all over again? Stupid kid, he would have to come along and point that out before I saw it for myself. Too smart for his too big britches that make him look like a fugitive from grade school.'

It was a quiet meal and it was Amy who opened the subject again. "He doesn't live in a tepee, Father."

"No, I don't imagine many of them do anymore."

"Them? Who is 'them'?"

"The local Indians."

"Well, I don't think he's very much an Indian. Or if he is then it isn't a thing that has hurt him a whole lot is it? I mean he is so knowledgeable about so many things that are actually useful or interesting and not like a lot of that pap they feed us in school. You know, I've never before met anyone my own age who is so pleasantly entertaining."

Thinking of the monosyllabic replies he had gotten from the kid at first and then the long offerings of opinionated advice later, Ruff wondered. For an eighteen year old attractive and unattached girl he must spin his hat around to a different slant.

Of course Buck alone would win her over the way she loves horses—a trait she did not inherit from him or from Libby—it must be an inclination all her own.

"I suppose they have a bigger, better house than ours?"

"No, not bigger, it's quite small actually and made of logs but there's just Eddy and his mother living in it so it's all they need. Actually, Eddy sleeps in the loft of a building they use to store saddles, harness and some grain—you wouldn't believe the marvellous smells in it—mice too, I'm afraid, but he has a cat that—." She stopped there because her father had exploded in a fit of choking and coughing.

Even through the agony and near fainting of trying to get a breath of air down a windpipe fighting to rid itself of bread crumbs Ruff knew it was a good thing he couldn't speak right then. Never slow or shy about stating his feelings loudly, he had blown up just once too often at Libby and that painful memory made him determined to do better with his daughter. The last thing he wanted was to alienate her too. These breathless, speechless minutes that felt like hours to him were probably a blessing not even a little bit disguised.

Finally he managed, "how"—another fit of coughing—"d'you know all that?"

"Why, I've been over twice now to visit them, if you didn't know that then you haven't been listening very closely to me."

"No, I haven't been listening closely enough to hear the thoughts you have never put to voice."

"Don't give me that, Father, you get your nose in your newspaper or a magazine and you don't hear a word I say."

"Then that's the time to tell me what you don't want me to know isn't it?"

"Of course it is."

Just like him she was bristling—just like her mother too. Poor kid—she has a double dose of it in her blood. Maybe Libby's 'gangster' deserves her—maybe the kid deserves her—she'd

34

shoot down his high and mighty airs. Ruff deeply resented the kid being right about that gully.

"I'm sorry I flew off the handle Amy. Would you like to tell me about it now while I have no newspaper in my hands?"

"Not if you are just going to complain next week that I didn't."

"No, I'll not be doing that. How'd you get to his place anyway?"

"The first time I went over he brought a borrowed horse for me. Then day before yesterday we went in the car, after all, he had to run a test drive to make the final adjustments to it."

"So now the gasoline tank is empty! Lucky you didn't run out somewhere along the way."

"Now Father, Eddy is a better planner than that—he had a can of gas at his place that he poured in—you probably have more gas now than before."

"Hmf! Where does he live?" Ruff was still thinking southward.

"Just about due west from here and not so far away if you go straight across the hills, about two miles he says but twice that far by the road. You go south from here to the main road then west almost to the river hill then north on a bush road—an old logging road I suppose though Eddy says part of it used to be the old Kalispell to Fort Steele wagon trail and even had a telegraph line along it and he still picks up a bit of the wire now and then."

"I've heard of that."

"Then you swing a loop to the left and climb about half way up the hill and there they are. It's a secluded little bench where you could walk by a hundred yards away on any side and not notice a thing."

Ruff was still having trouble with one thing she had said, "he showed you where he sleeps did he?"

"Sure," she let a second or two drag by, "that was the first time I was over and actually his sister showed me that—Eddy had to leave to go to his job at the mill. She showed me her place too—up on top of the hill—I had lunch with her. I suppose it's a nice location and the house is big enough—two stories—but it's very poorly built. I'll bet it's harder to heat in winter than this one and you know all about that."

"If Eddy had to leave then how'd you get home?"

"I walked home. Eddy said I could take the horse and he would pick it up later but I elected to walk. Like I said, it's not far straight across country, I could have found my own way in the dark but his sister walked along with me because she is the kind who likes to be sure—then she walked back to her home."

"All alone?"

"Don't worry about her Dad, she knows her way around the hills here almost as well as Eddy does. She has a gun and judging by the way she carries it I think she knows how to use it. Her mother took care of her little boys while she brought me home." Amy's eyes glittered, "her youngest son is under a year old and the oldest is nearly four years—she's sixteen—two years younger than I am. "

Ruff had never known this house to be so quiet—not even in the dead of night—as it was over the next long minute.

"You're pulling my leg Amy. Getting even for that thoughtless comment I made to you."

"Yes, that's right but I am telling you the truth," again she paused to let him think the worst, "just not quite all of it. Actually the oldest boy is her step son—her husband's by a previous marriage."

"Amy, hold it right there!"

"Why, what's wrong?"

"Because you are ringing bells all over in my head—alarm bells! This must be Percy Stuart's bunch that you are talking about. The ones who live on Apple Tree Hill."

"Yes, I guess that's right. What's wrong with that?"

"A lot!"

"Such as?"

"Well—Percy himself seems a pretty decent sort—he works for Simon too—but he's gone and gotten mixed up with a bad bunch there. I hate to have to tell you this but that little girl is not married to him. He probably should be put in jail for that alone even if he is innocent of everything else."

"I don't like this, Father, you're not making much sense. That 'little girl' you are talking about is taller than I am and I'm very glad she was not in my class in school because if she had been there would have been no boys for the rest of us—they would all have been fawning around her. What do you mean—'not married'—how could she not be married to her hus—to the man she lives—I mean to her baby's father?"

"I know, it sounds far fetched and I've always tried to take camp gossip with a grain of salt but the story seems to amount to the same no matter where it comes from so there must be some truth to it."

"Since you have gone this far without saying anything believable I think you had better tell me all of it."

"Yes. But I've never paid that much attention to gossip. I wish now that I had since you seem to have gotten mixed up with them."

"Mixed up! Mixed up? Eddy is okay! His sister Hettie and his mother Reb are okay too. Quit beating around the bush the way Mother does—it's not like you."

"You're right. It's just that suddenly I feel that I know so little and I wish I knew more. But, from what I've heard it would seem that girl's father—Eddy's father—was an old Indian," he paused as he remembered Eddy's definition, "or part Indian, who was a known raider in the old days—a killer from ambush and a thief. He was known only as Mica—nothing else—no family name. He gave his daughter to Percy as a gift after driving the legal wife half crazy with fear of him and forcing her to leave the country."

Amy had paled. "But she left her son behind so she must not have feared for him."

"They might have made her leave without him for all I know. Some say they killed her and just said that she left."

"Stop it! If you don't know it don't say it."

"I have to because you are asking so I have to tell you what I've heard."

"Well, it can't be nearly as bad as you are making out because there is no feeling of evil among them at all. To me they seem like perfectly normal people—just a little backward and shy from living such isolated lives. But then nearly everyone around this neck of the woods seems backward compared to the city people I've gotten used to. You too!"

"That may well be but he stole the parts he used to fix my car, Amy. I wasn't going to tell you that but I guess I have to."

"He did not 'steal' them! He has played a joke on your precious Mr. Simon who has more money than all the rest of us added together and someday when Mr. Simon is in the right mood Eddy will tell him in a way that will have him scratching his head then laughing when he figures it out."

"So you knew he was putting in parts that didn't belong either to him or to me."

"Of course I did. As soon as he found what was wrong he told me where he would get new ones of whatever it was and I laughed and laughed when I heard the car running so good the next day."

"That makes you as guilty of theft as Eddy and I are."

"Oh Dad, talk sense, what you have been insinuating all along about Eddy and his father amounts to the same as if you were to go out and shoot someone then I should be hung along with you."

Ruff stared at his daughter a moment then smiled a little. "No. What I am saying is that if I go out and shoot someone— then your future husband had better watch his back."

Amy smiled too but not much. "Yes, there is a difference isn't there."

They were silent as she collected the dishes and silverware from the table. "I meant it when I said we have to get to town for some things and now we can go since the car runs so good."

"Ah, I'm afraid not, or at least we can't buy much. I can charge what I need up the road here and my bill will be paid but I have no money to buy elsewhere."

"Oh. I see."

Ruff cringed inwardly for he knew what she saw. While Corrie's wages paid for his purchases, now that they lived apart, she did not share the remaining cash with him. Actually she hadn't for some time now.

Later in the evening and hundreds of miles to the west a man sat alone at his table sipping coffee to end the meal that had been delivered from the dinning room down on the ground floor. He reached inside his vest to a hidden pocket for a folded page of paper which he opened and flattened between his cup and the untouched desert. He did not read any of the hand written message on it—once had been enough to ignite a cold anger that heated and smouldered as he sensed all that was written between the lines. On the back there was a rough drawn map and now he turned the page over to it and compared it to a larger map that was spread out on one end of the table.

'My road map may be a bit outdated but there seems to be no practical way to drive from here to there without jogging down through Washington State. And part of Idaho too.'

'If that girl thinks I am going to drop everything and drive five or six hundred miles to find her—— .'

Chapter 5

Sure footed little Buck was falling. Going down so sudden that Eddy had no chance to swing clear. The ground was coming up fast and he knew it was going to hurt.

In the tiny loft of the saddle and harness shed Eddy sat up with such a jerk that he sent tremors all through the upper reaches of the small frame building. It was dark yet—totally dark.

"That dream again," he breathed in relief as he rubbed the pain out of the left side of his face. His left foot hurt too so he flexed it until it stopped throbbing. There was no blood and no injury so he stretched out again hoping to sleep until dawn.

"Well. I see you finally got yourself on the right track here but why don't you use a team and a walking plough? You could do this about ten or twenty, maybe even a hundred, times faster than with that grubhoe."

Ruff straightened slowly. His back hurt and it wasn't all from bending to his work—this kid had everything it took to irritate him.

"It might help if you'd make a little noise as you come sneaking up on me."

"Mister Ruff! With all due respect. Was I sneaking up on you you wouldn't ever know it." Perhaps unconsciously Eddy's hand brushed the stock of his saddle gun. "When you get your head down you just plain seem to go deaf."

"If you're so smart, then you already know I don't have any horses. I've got a riding plough but a walking plough is something I don't ever plan to own." Ruff had seen that fond and intimate hand stroke along the rifle stock and it sent a shiver down his spine. Now that he knew who this kid was he was even more uneasy with these silent approaches. That keen eyed interest of the little buckskin now seemed worrisome too. Watching eagerly for the bullets to fly? Just how much like his father might this boy be?

"Yeah. I've noticed. How you expect to pull that riding plough without horses? With the Studebaker?"

"I plan to get a tractor."

"Oh. Like that Fordson old Chrysler has?"

"Right. But I was thinking Case."

"Only Case I ever saw was a steam tractor and pretty big too. You don't want one of them."

"Why not?"

"Well. Number one. You ain't got enough farm to run one in a circle without your neighbours gettin' mad at you. And number two—you'd have the whole country up in smoke if the thing didn't blow up and kill you first. I mean—anybody that can't file down a set of ignition points—better leave steam power to somebody else."

"To the likes of you, I suppose." No attempt today at proper grammar Ruff surmised. Like both Eddy and Buck he was more comfortable with this return to normal.

"Why sure. Reckon I could figure one out."

To his immense surprise Ruff found he was inclined to accept that vain statement as the simple truth—yes—this kid probably could 'figure one out'. "They make smaller ones too that run on gasoline or distillate. Like Chrysler's."

"What's distillate? Coal oil?"

"Close enough I guess." Ruff was certainly not about to admit that he didn't know for sure either.

"Or maybe that mixture of gasoline and used engine oil I've seen Chrysler pour into his?"

Ruff knew nothing of that so he simply ignored the question. "I don't have any neighbours so I guess I can wheel as big a circle as I want."

"You got neighbours now whether you want them or not."

"What? Since when and who?"

"That timekeeper guy from the mill," the kid thumbed in the direction of the sawmill, "and his brother that took over as flunky when the last one quit."

"So that's who is flunky now. She didn't tell me." But then he hadn't asked either and had timed his visits to off hours for both cook and flunky. There was a scary gap in his understanding of his young wife and though he wasn't sure when it had started it had definitely widened during the time they had both lived in the cookhouse. It might have started about the time he had tried explaining to Corrie the better way Libby had for doing something. He couldn't remember now what that had been but he sure remembered Corrie's reaction. It was a mistake he had vowed never to make again. Nor did it help any whenever he began talking about something that Libby would have known and understood but went back to before Corrie's time as an adult.

"Floyd ain't a bad sort, Ruff. But he will be if he takes too many lessons from his older brother."

"Errol must be trustworthy or Simon wouldn't have given him the job of timekeeper. Pretty responsible position—he must do about everything that's done on paper around there except to sign the cheques. I think he is tame enough"

"Yeah. Maybe. But it's a job with temptations and opportunities and when I look at Errol I think of coyote—opportunist—and I never would trust a coyote around my henhouse. Not even a tame one."

"That's Simon's worry and I guess he will be watching over things close enough. Why do you say they are neighbours of mine?"

"Well. I reckon you wouldn't notice seein' as you ain't never around your place no more since you started work on this ditch thing. They have pegged out and taken up a chunk of land that joins your place. It lays along your south side and goes half a mile on from there so it must be a quarter section—a hundred and sixty acres—same as yours."

"No kidding! Now why on earth would they want all that? I can't see either of them out working on a farm."

"Nope. You said that right. But it could be because if you get water down to your place then all of a sudden their place is worth a whole lot more than they paid for it. Which I reckon was next to nothing same as you would have paid for yours. Then they got something to sell."

"I'm not making the ditch big enough to carry water for two places so theirs might not be worth so much."

"Aw. There's always an optimist out there who might not notice that at first or might think he could make the ditch bigger and get enough water for his needs too."

"By the time the people over at the base of the mountain take what they want there's not much left to come out here except in the spring runoff while the snow up high is melting."

"Well. Then I reckon that's the time to bring in the customer to look at it—while the creek is bank full."

Ruff had to agree and grinned ruefully. "That's the time to sell any land around here—while it looks fresh and green from the spring thaw and early rains. Sure not in July or August. Not in June of this year either unless it clouds up and does some raining soon"

"Long about the time the boys over by the mountains get their hay down to dry the monsoons will blow in. Always rains in June—just not enough some years."

"You talk like you've been around a lot longer than you look to have been."

"Well. The old timers got it all stored away in their heads— just have to be quiet and listen."

"That right?" 'You can be quiet?' "And what do they say about this trend we seem to be in toward hotter drier summers and dry warm winters?"

"Been through it all before—they can tell you what years the crops and range grass all burned up for want of rain. Can tell you too about winters that started in September and didn't end till May—times when forty below was a mild morning. Been times when various ranchers might of wandered through where we stand right now only in November on snowshoes looking for stock to see if they was still alive and wondering how to get them home or how to get some hay out to them. Other winters with not a scrap of snow and no rain the following summer. Then you could stand on either side of this little valley and not be able to see across to the other side for smoke from forest fires. Same ranchers riding around looking for stock and wondering if they was still alive or if they had died of suffocation or been burned up."

"You paint a bleak picture—makes me glad I have no ambitions toward cattle or horses—makes a tractor look real good. I like the thought of just shutting it down and walking away from it without having to feed or water it or catch and harness it in the morning."

Buck stamped a foot and tossed his head impatiently then intensified his careful inspection of Ruff who had taken one step back. The kid grinned.

"That's impossible," Ruff exclaimed, "he couldn't have understood me! Could he?"

"Nope. Not word for word but he knows darn well you are picking on him and his kind. Now he's gonna be looking forward to watching you tinkering on your tractor out in the field when the ignition takes on a cold or the carburetor gets stuffed up. Or maybe when you pop a gear in the transmission or bust a hind axle. Tractors need care too—just like Studebakers."

"Maybe I'll hire you to take care of it for me."

"Sure. That'll work. Got the money to pay me?"

"No!"

"Thought so."

Buck decided it was time to go but the kid stopped him by letting a hand stray over the edge of the saddle to touch one fingertip against the little horse.

"But. That's neither here nor there 'cause sometimes I work cheap or even for free if I like a person. Or maybe just if I like what they are doing."

That offer hung in the air between them. The kid wondering if Ruff was smart enough to understand it as intended and Ruff wondering why this kid had to speak in riddles half the time and so bluntly at other times. Was it an offer? How cheap?

Don't ask.

"I could sure use some help to build the flume. I don't know about the pay.

"We'll figure it out as it comes. Don't see no problem."

"What about your job at the woodpile?"

"Well. Looks like a few days yet before you'll be ready to start on that flume so I will whack up a pile of wood at the kitchen and change my schedule so I'll be free. As long as it stays hot so only the cook is burning wood then I ain't gonna be pressed. You can get boards for the water box?"

"I can get the boards." But Ruff frowned, he'd get them and the price would be taken from Corrie's pay. She wouldn't like it he knew but she had bought in to this outfit when she married him—so—too bad.

"Got spikes and nails too?."

"A few but I'll have to find more I guess." He frowned again mentally adding up Corrie's earnings and subtracting boards and nails plus the regular store bill too. The result didn't look so good.

"You know?"

"Yes?"

"If we can haul them with the Studebaker I know where we can get some boards that might do the trick. I reckon we can get nails and spikes too at the same time."

"Where would that be?"

"Down at Dolph's camp. Still lots of good pickings there if we get right at it before it's all gone."

"That still belongs to Dolph Lumber doesn't it?"

"Seeing as nobody else has bought and paid for it I reckon it does but old Dolph don't want it no more. They're plumb gone now and they ain't coming back. Last time I went by there was still lots of long wide boards on the roof of one of the bigger buildings. They won't be there for long though. Now that I have thought out loud about it we better drop everything else and go get them. They'll be dry and will swell up to hold water real good—not like the fresh green stuff you would get from Simon."

"Yes, I was a bit worried about that. We'll go see what we can find as soon as I get logs in place for the sills and have all the uprights built."

"Nope. We'll go tomorrow. Now that I have said it out loud somebody else will be thinking the same thing so we got to beat them to it. I'll come real early and do the woodpile then I'll ride straight to Dolph's and meet you there about the same time you usually start here."

"You can be there that early?"

"Sure. I don't slumber away till the sun comes up like you do. I'll be there or arriving shortly. You got hammers and wrecking bars?"

"I have a couple of hammers and a crowbar."

Throw them in an' I'll bring my own nail puller—I got a good one—brings the nail out straight most every time."

"Alright. Say, Eddy."

Again Eddy stopped the little horse without seeming to have done so.

"You'll be riding right past my place early so why not stop in for breakfast?"

"Now. That sounds like the way to do it. Sure, I'll stop in and I thank you for the invite."

"You can leave your horse there and go with me in the car." 'Now why did I go and ask him to eat with us! Oh well, it will let me see how he and Amy react to each other. Which may or may not be the same as when I'm not there.'

"Aw. No. It ain't far from your place to Dolph's. Me and Buck can get there about as fast as you can."

This time Eddy made no effort to stop his horse whose impatience had started him on the move again.

Through the night while Eddy slept and hundreds of miles to the west, a black McLaughlin with a single occupant cleared customs at ten minutes to midnight and sped south toward Seattle.

Chapter 6

Breakfast the next morning was an eye opener for Ruff. Normally he only saw his daughter when he came home in late afternoon since after reading by the gas lamp past midnight she was seldom up till after he was gone in the morning. Someday he might find a way to talk to her about the high cost of lamp gas but right now he was just too glad to have her at home. She was, however, up early enough this morning to take command of the breakfast making and by the time the kid arrived she had the table set and waiting for him. Ruff himself felt merely incidental to the scene. And the way she wore her shirt! Barely legal for public appearance in his opinion. Of course the kitchen was already hot and that "accidental" peek of bare skin above her belt when she bent just so wasn't for the public—it was for the kid.

Eddy was in love! That was plain to see in the adoring look on his face as he followed her every movement. Ruff had to say everything twice—once to get the kid's attention and again to get the message across. Only when Eddy saw there were no more pancakes being offered did a minor irritation cross his face but that cleared like magic as Amy lay her hand on his shoulder and leaned over him—altogether too closely over him—to fill his cup with coffee.

Amy was not in love! That too was plain to see. Ruff didn't know whether to laugh or to gnash his teeth in angry frustration as she teased Eddy unmercifully. Her mother would be shocked and furious—with him too for not knowing how to stop it. He became so bound up in thoughts of how angry Libby would be that he failed to understand that what she was trying to say was directed more to him than to Eddy.

She's only eighteen! Where, he wondered, has she learned to act like this? Once again he felt sorry for the kid and did eventually rescue him by almost literally dragging him outside to aim him south on his horse. Ruff considered going back to tell Amy what he thought of her performance but then reconsidered—'chickened out,' he had to admit—and climbed into the car to follow the kid southward.

Eddy beat him to Dolph's abandoned lumber camp and he was all business as they removed boards from the roof of one of the larger buildings. All morning they worked at it pulling the nails and spikes slowly and with great care so as to not bend them or to crack the boards. Nails went into one bucket and spikes into another—buckets the kid hunted for and found somewhere around the old buildings because Ruff had not thought to bring any.

"I feel like a criminal here tearing someone else's property apart."

"Aw. Don't work up no sweat over it, Ruff. If they decide they still want it then it's their own fault that it's gone home with us cause they shouldn't have left temptation dangling like candy in front of we kids."

"Still, it just doesn't feel right."

"Yeah. I see you watching over your shoulder half the time. What you looking for—the B.C. Provincial boys in uniform?"

"I guess so. Or the owner coming with a gun."

"Never! You got a long wait coming. About now they are hundreds, maybe thousands of miles away spending the money they made here."

"I heard they went broke."

"Naw. Not this outfit. Chuck figures they did real good here. If they found a way to go broke then I reckon they made money on that too."

"Chuck, who?"

"My neighbour Chuck. Him and his wife Myrtle own the old place at the top of the Dorr hill. You know both of them."

"Oh, sure, I know who you mean."

"That's them. A fair bit of what's missing here now has already walked it's way over to their place so don't get to thinking you are breaking a new colt."

"I think the saying is actually 'breaking new ground'."

"Yep. That's what I said." With no change in tone Eddy went on, "we got company coming, Ruff. Now, it ain't the cops and it ain't the owner so don't go running off to hide nor to the car for your gun. It's just an old cowboy out looking for his cows."

Ruff, alarmed despite Eddy's reassurance, looked wildly down the road then the other way too but saw no one. After a few seconds spent bracing himself for the embarrassment of discovery he heard sounds of a horse coming from one side. He looked that way to find that a man about his own age on a sorrel saddle horse was almost within talking range. An "old" cowboy? Well, perhaps from the viewpoint of a teenager.

"You must have x-ray vision to recognise him through the trees."

"Aw. No. I saw enough of the horse to know who it was. He nearly always rides that sorrel mare."

The newcomer rode up closer than Ruff felt was necessary before stopping to look them over.

"Morning Jim. Or has it slipped around to afternoon?"

Jim glanced toward the sun, "reckon it's just about there, Ed, and it sure feels like middle of the day—can't say I remember such a hot spell in May. How about that! I'm a poet and I didn't even know it."

"Aw, Jim. I've known that ever since I looked at your feet." They both laughed but Ruff had no idea what the joke was.

Jim, who had been sizing Ruff up, now nodded as if finally introduced, "how doin', Ruff."

"Just fine, Jim." Surprised at being known by a man he couldn't remember ever having seen before it came out almost squeaky yet sounded defensive, "you too I hope."

"Oh, sure. I could complain—probably should—but it never seems to help much so I won't waste time on it. Seen any cows in your travels, Ed?"

Eddy had seen quite a few cows over the last while but he knew which one Jim was after. "Nope, I ain't seen her since that day you was looking at her by that slough over east of here."

"Well, I suppose by now she is either on the mend or has died but if she's down then I'd like to find her calf and take it home."

Still uncomfortable with being known to a man who was a stranger to him Ruff stole glances while trying to seem not to. Black hair under a sweat stained, once upon a time tan coloured felt hat, the man was almost as skinny as Eddy but his shoulders were broad and his arms muscular. Under the shade of his hat brim he was as dark skinned as the kid though it might all be sun tan like it is for Amy. 'He must be from one of the families over along the mountains.' Like the kid he had not shaved this morning but unlike the kid he really should have. He too wore jeans only his fit properly and tucked into them was a light grey shirt with almost invisible, thread thin, vertical blue lines—it was patched extensively along one arm. His boots were heavy leather, work or walking types and only the tip of the toes were stuck into the stirrups. No money for fancy riding boots Ruff guessed.

"I've been to every water hole between home and here and I'll check them again on my way back but if you see her, Ed, or her calf, maybe you could slide the word to me."

51

"Sure will, Jim, I'll keep an eye open."

Jim, about to leave, paused, "doing a nice careful job of salvaging those boards. Didn't know there was much of anything useful left here. Might come over with the wagon and get a few of those too. Or do you guys need all that's left?"

"No. Reckon we will have enough from this one slope of the roof. Wouldn't you say so, Ruff?"

"Yes, I'm sure this will be more than we need."

Jim nodded, "see you around then, Ed—Ruff."

The kid raised one hand giving a half wave, half salute so Ruff did the same and felt foolish for it.

"We should've asked him to eat with us, we've got lots." But he had waited until the stranger was out of sight before suggesting it.

"No. If he stops to eat at all he will eat alone and on top of a hill where he can see all around. He don't ever stop often to talk or have so much to say—reckon he was plumb curious or we wouldn't have seen him at all today."

"How did he know who I am? I'm sure I've never met him before."

"The car."

"Oh. Same as you knew him way off by his horse."

"Sure."

"What's wrong with his cow?"

"Broken leg."

"Ouch. Means shooting her I guess."

"Well. One might think so. But he says he had one like this before—front leg, below the knee—that healed up okay—just a little crooked. Course that one he had at home in the corral so this might be different. Just the fact that he can't find her is good news—means she is on the move or at least not smelling bad yet."

"Sure makes me glad I have no cows—I wouldn't want to have to watch something like that and make the decision he might have to."

"It's just a cow."

"It's a living creature the same as us."

"Not quite the same. Otherwise a fellow could put a splint on that leg and tell her to take it easy for a spell. For us a busted bone is an inconvenience sure enough but for pretty much any animal type it's an open letter of invitation to the coyotes."

"Even so—I have almost come to think it a cruelty just to own an animal."

"Hey! You better have a talk with little Buck here. See what he says about that. Specially in winter time while I'm forking some nice green hay to him."

"If he had a broken leg you would shoot him."

"I would too. And the cruelty and cryin' would not all be one sided if I had to do that, Ruff. Old Ma Nature's laws can be pretty tough. Dang it, that poet stuff of Jim's is plumb contagious."

"What did you mean by that crack about his feet?"

"You never heard that before?"

"I don't think so."

"Man! Where have you been? That must be about the third oldest one in the book—I knew he was a poet because of his feet—they're Longfellows."

Ruff waited a bit. "That's it?"

"Reckon you don't know many poet types."

"I guess not."

"I think we better check out that lunch I saw you loading into the car—see if it's still with us or has dried up and blew away in this heat. We can find some shade over there where we can look out over the lake"

"Okay." Ruff wasn't hungry but having watched Eddy at breakfast he suspected that hunger and appeasing it were the number one and number two foremost instincts with the kid.

"I'd hardly call that pothole slough a lake."

"It's water. Enough to get wet in if you slipped and fell flat. In a dry land like this that makes it a lake in my book."

Ruff chuckled as he went for the lunch box even though, other than Eddy's definition of a lake, he hadn't seen or heard much of anything funny yet today. Being caught vandalising this place—even if by another vandal—had been a bad experience and definitely not funny. Too honest for his own good! He had been told that more than once, for that matter, more than once by Libby alone. He should have known he would be caught. And the boards still had to be hauled to the site of the flume—practically in Simon's back yard and almost in the shadows of his lumber piles. His car was running on stolen parts and he had accepted the help of an obviously practised and unrepentant thief. The son of another thief, raider, bandit, and murderer too if rumours held water. Somehow this help will have to be paid for! Ruff shuddered, 'Amy—Amy—you are a jewel but why do you attract this kind?'

"Had all you want?"

"What's that? Oh, yes, go ahead." Eddy whisked away the last sandwich before Ruff remembered he hadn't had any at all yet. He poured more tea from his thermos and wished he had a bicarbonate of soda instead.

Eddy, on the other hand, still suffering from that skimpy breakfast and seeing no more than starvation rations in the lunch box, chewed every bite of this last sandwich long and carefully hoping to fool his stomach into thinking it had been fed. He had seen Ruff's preoccupation and knew the man had eaten nothing but that was the other's problem—not his.

"That's a nice looking rifle you carry on the back seat of your car. What is it?"

".30-40 Krag." The man who would never willingly shoot a living creature brightened with pride at mention of his gun."

"Never heard of one before."

"Not surprised, it's the only one I've ever run onto. Got to go across the Line to get ammunition for it so I reload my own."

"Most of us do. Only way to keep table meat down to a reasonable price an' still be able to shoot a stump now and then."

54

"Why'd you shoot a stump?"

"Aw. Just a way to admit that I miss now and then. Or shoot at a target about twice a year."

"Let's shoot at a target now."

"Why for?"

"Because I want to see what you carry in that saddle scabbard and what you can do with it."

"Aw. It ain't nothing fancy. A hard used one that I got for an easy trade."

"Well, get it and I'll get mine, we'll see who can be first to hit one of those sticks floating at the far side of the lake." 'An "easy trade"? Spelled the same as "stolen"? Not for me to worry about. I might not know of many poets but I'll show him what shooting is.'

"That's an odd looking rig. One of those Savage, hammerless carbines?"

"It is so. It's not what I pack when I go on foot for some serious hunting in the brush but I kind of like it. Fits good in my saddle scabbard and, like me, it's different than most." Eddy smiled his satisfaction with that thought.

They sat again on the ground alongside the very empty lunch box. Ruff aimed across the lake at something but didn't fire.

"Trade guns for first shot?"

"Aw. No. Don't think so."

"Why not?"

"Well. I don't know anything about yours an' you don't know anything about mine."

"What's to know? I can tell you to draw a fine bead with mine—you can tell me how with yours." It pleased Ruff to see the kid uncomfortable and uncertain as much as to feel the confidence that came to himself as he handled his own rifle.

"Well. Mine's kind of hair trigger. Don't generally let anybody else touch it in case it goes off too soon on them. Might cause an accident."

"Those things don't come hair triggered from the factory—you must've done something to it."

"That's so. I took it apart and filed here and there till I had it about right. Done that with all my guns to some extent—this one maybe a little more than I should have."

"How come?"

"Well. I kind of like them to go off while I'm still thinking about it. Don't like them hanging fire while supper runs off over the ridge."

"Hm. Makes it kind of dangerous."

"Too true. Just what I was telling you. All guns got to be thought of as dangerous—this one just a little more so. Once I got it loaded and ready you don't want to startle me even a little bit or it goes off all by it's lonesome if I got my finger anywhere near the trigger. It's kind of like a good horse—it runs on thought waves as much as by touch."

"Okay, I'll shoot first then. See that sort of square piece of wood floating near the far shore? Just about in line with that big crooked, limby, Ponderosa."

Eddy made a show of squinting, "just barely."

"I'll try to hit right under it's front edge and lift it out of the water." Ruff, sitting with elbows on knees, aimed carefully—held steady—then raised his head to look again at the target. After a few seconds he aimed once more and this time the little square of wood shot four feet into the air on top a geyser of water. The echoes of the shot rolled around and back and forth from the timbered hills surrounding the lake. Eddy stared wordless as the circle of ripples widened, one half coming across the lake toward them and the far half destroying themselves in confusion on the shore beyond.

"Your turn."

"Um. No! There's no use. I could never do that. I'd be lucky to hit the lake."

"Oh, go ahead. See how close you can come."

"No. I'd just be wasting a shot."

"So what? I wasted one."

"That wasn't wasted! That was good shooting."

"Oh, come on, you're always bragging about shooting your supper to drag home—now let's see what you can really do."

"But. That's different."

"How can it be different? It's still aim and shoot."

"No! It ain't. What you did was aim and shoot and you showed me something I know is far beyond anything I can ever expect to do."

"It's all aim and shoot, just takes a little practice."

"Well. I reckon like you say—it takes a little practice. But it also takes a good eye, a steady hand and a pile of skill. I ain't got that kind of skill so I have to do it my way."

"And what is 'your way'."

"Well now. I never before had to think about it but I reckon you could call it 'point and shoot'. You know—point your finger and you know you are pointing to the right spot—point your gun and know in your mind that you are pointing to the right spot just like with the finger. Don't waste no time thinking about it or you'll miss. Maybe the gun has to do it's share too but you have to know—strongly—in your mind and heart that you are going to hit. You and the gun have to be thinking the same way."

"Yeah, sure. I've heard this one before. You're just another one of those jokers who can't hit a big cardboard box at fifty steps with witnesses standing around but you can drop a running deer with one shot at four hundred yards as long as no one is watching."

"I reckon."

"You reckon what?"

"I reckon I couldn't hit a box at fifty paces."

"Ha ha, but you could get the deer at four hundred I suppose."

"Well. You know, Ruff. It has to be admitted. Half that anyhow."

"Sure." 'Why was I ever afraid of this loudmouthed fake', Ruff wondered. His good humour, sorely beaten and battered this day, was much restored. "If you won't show me what you can do with that piece of scratched wood and rusty iron then let me try it. I'll be careful of your 'hair trigger'." Ruff reached for Ed's rifle as he spoke and the kid reluctantly let him have it.

"It might be scratched but it ain't rusty. I've taken good care of it but it did get some tossing around earlier in it's life. Just watch where you point it once you work the lever and get one up."

"Sure." Ruff gingerly pushed the lever down until he could see that the firing chamber was empty then he ran it on to the end of it's travel all the while peering into the rifle's opening action as the bullet came up. "Cylindrical magazine—never did like them—too easy to freeze up in the wet and cold. Hot looking little cartridge though. What is it, 250-3000?"

"You've banged the hammer's head square on with the nail."

'Should be a good shooting little gun—feels good—but lever action is never accurate so I don't think you'll ever pull off any long range shots with this one."

"What's wrong with lever action?"

"Too much give in the mechanism when you fire. Not firm and strong like a bolt action. But—we'll see—." He closed the action, started to raise the rifle but flinched as it fired slamming the stock against his shoulder hard enough to hurt since he hadn't yet tightened up on it. The bullet plowed into the lake half way across.

"Whoa! Man, you weren't kidding when you said it was hair trigger! I sure wasn't ready for that. Lucky I didn't get one of my own toes."

"I warned you. If you can feel the cool of steel radiating off the trigger at your finger joint then back off cause you are getting too close. Try another."

"Yes, I will."

Ruff worked the lever again once more watching inside the action as he did so. This time he kept his finger outside the trigger guard until he was ready to shoot. The flake of wood rocked in the ripples set off by the bullet's strike—two feet low and equally to the right.

"Not bad—not bad at all—a whole lot better than I expected, but you sure won't pull off any long range kills with this thing. Still—a little more front bead in the sight and—." Without asking he levered in another round, aimed and fired again. This time the the bullet hit four feet low and six feet to the right.

"Ah ha! You have a problem here, Ed. Either the barrel is damaged inside or it's not bedded right in the stock. It's creeping off farther as the barrel expands with the warmth of each shot." He opened the action to eject the empty casing but stuck a finger inside to roll the next cartridge back so he could close it with the chamber empty and held the trigger as he did so. He turned the gun over to examine it before handing it back. By then Ed had retrieved all three ejected casings and slid them into empty belt loops.

"I could fix it for you—probably just needs a little sanding on the stock and adjusting of the sights."

"No!"

"No? I could make it shoot a lot better for you."

"I don't want it fiddled with."

"Why not? You sure can't hit anything with it like that."

"I get along just fine with it the way it is. Might take months to get back on speaking terms with it if—- in fact—here comes my kind of target now."

Ruff looked where the kid was but saw nothing except a raven flitting behind the trees beyond the far shore of the lake perhaps drawn by the shooting but keeping a safe distance away. Farther actually than the chip of wood was. From the corner of his vision he saw the kid raise his faulty rifle, work the lever, aim and fire all in one swift motion. Across the lake, beyond the closest trees as it crossed the small gap between two of them, the raven burst into an expanding puff of feathers that fell to the opposite hillside.

Ruff's face went pasty pale and his jaw fell slack. Once again he felt a desperate need for a glass of soda water.

"Aw. I'm sorry Ruff. I shouldn't of done that." Whether Eddy was apologising for making the shot or for killing the bird was hard to say. "But you made me mad."

Chapter 7

A my watched her father as he and Ed prepared to leave on whatever mission it was that they were bent upon but she stood well back from the window where she would not be seen. If he returned to the house when Ed left she would go to her room and close the door. Confronted with that closed door she was confident that no matter how angry he was he would go away and tell himself he would talk to her later. By the time 'later' presented itself the edge would be gone from his anger and he might say nothing at all. She had expected his anger and had deliberately goaded it as far as she dared. He had to come to the understanding that she was no longer his 'little baby girl'—that she was now a grown up person with her own ideas and plans for her future.

Eddy—dear, unsuspecting and willing to be used, Eddy—who to begin with had been an unexpected complication because his attentions were unwanted, now seemed the perfect vehicle to bring about that understanding. She had come to like Ed—a lot actually—he was so easy to like that she would have to be on guard against liking him too much. But he was such an impossible suitor—her visits to his home had determined that very quickly. Some local girl might be happy to live on deer meat and garden produce along with what little could be bought from a wood cutting job—but not her. She sensed that her father's opinions of Eddy were about the same if not quite as strong so if she brushed often enough against him in her father's presence he would soon be glad to have just about any other man arrive on the scene. Especially one as handsome, pleasant and obviously wealthy as the one who was going to show up soon.

As the one who had darned well better show up soon if he was really as serious about her as he made out.

Reece. Her mother called him a gangster, a wannabe mafia mobster, and anything else uncomplimentary that she could think of. Just because he owned a hotel and was older than Amy by more than ten years. Twenty nine wasn't 'old' even if just a year ago she would have thought it was. That's about how long ago she had first become aware that the handsome man in the fancy car had picked her for special attention.

Walking home from school with girl friends they had one day realized that the big black car with the lone male occupant was parked where he could watch them too often to be accidental. Having no clue as to which of them he was watching they sauntered more elegantly and though they didn't know it—more self consciously. Except Amy who walked as she had always walked because having caught the man's eye, she knew that she was the one selected.

He made no effort to approach any closer than that until almost a year later as she neared the end of grade twelve. That eventual approach was made possible by her arranging to be alone at the right time and place so he had only to reach across to open the passenger side door and she had slid right in and smiled at him. By then she knew nearly as much about him as he had told her since. She knew that he owned one of the biggest and best hotels in that part of the city—that he owned it because he had inherited it when his father had been shot in a hunting accident. She knew that Reece had been accused of 'arranging' the accident, then, for lack of evidence, acquitted. She also knew it had all resurfaced when the man who had fired the accidental shot had been found with a broken neck in his burned out car at the bottom of a gully on a mountain road. Eventually it died away without further charges.

None of it bothered her and it wasn't only the money that swayed her though certainly it was a thing she had never had enough of in her life. Raised poor and poor yet she would not make the mistake of marrying poor as her mother had done. Eddy would be that mistake. One meeting of the eyes and she knew—this was the one she wanted—Reece was everything she could ask for.

The only problem with Reece was that he was not yet talking marriage. What he talked of was an apartment. The finest apartment on the top floor of his hotel where he would be her frequent visitor. There would be money too—lots of it—by the week in cash and a position as hostess that would be a cover for her presence. Some appearances to be made but little in the line of duties—more a sop for her mother's consumption.

The offer had neither shocked nor dismayed her. She had quickly become a city girl with an instinctive, beyond her age, understanding of men that let her read his intentions perfectly. It was partly why he was drawn more and more to her—she was hard to surprise and nearly impossible to frighten. At age seventeen, walking along the street with school chums he had seen her as 'his kind of woman' just as she had seen right through him at first eye contact and wanted him anyway. 'Love' had no part in it for either of them at that moment but the big car may have helped.

Amy felt no shame for the decisions she had come to nor any illusions as to the long term outcome of such an arrangement. Scuttlebutt had it that the apartment, which she had already been shown, was empty because the last occupant, also young and female, had been ejected with enough allowance to keep her quiet and drunk. To herself Amy finished the sentence with—'to make room for me'. She knew that if she agreed to the offer eventually it could end the same way for her when he found some fresh young girl to transfer his interest to. She knew that, as his attention waned, there might well be friends or business acquaintances sent for her to entertain. It sounded very exciting and laced with opportunity but was not what she wanted unless she simply could not get him to the altar. In that case, to have him for herself for as long as possible, she still had every intention of accepting the offer if that turned out to be the only way. But, when her time came to leave the apartment, the words 'drunk' and 'ejected' would not be a part of the explanation. Instead— the phrase—'the independently wealthy young woman who has quietly managed the social aspects of the establishment for the past (blank) years, has moved on to new challenges.'—might be used admiringly. No one would ever have to know how she felt inside.

The very first priority though was to become the legal mistress of the big house on the big lot on Marine Drive where he lived with his mother when not at the apartment. Or to some other suitable address if his mother objected to her presence. Once that position was gained she was confident the apartment would be let to regular tenants.

Amy had been caught flat footed though when her mother suddenly caught on to proceedings before she was ready to declare her intentions. Reece had arranged that she was to have a job when school ended—not at the hotel—and move away from home as step one. After a short while she would be promoted, moved to the apartment and her mother could whistle as she wished. There had been a dreadful argument—a real shouting match—and then her mother's plan to send her off to her father's where she would meet some decent young men. The argument had suddenly become one sided when quick witted Amy saw the situation as a perfect fit to her own plans.

Reece was pressing for an answer but Amy had not yet heard the right question. So she would knuckle under to her mother— go meekly to stay with her father on that horrible little homestead—write to Reece and if he came to rescue her—she had him! If he did not come—well—too bad—that might well be writing on the wall. She would then have to 'escape'—return to the Coast—she had enough for train fare—and take him up on the apartment and all that it meant. She would just have to work at it differently from there on. Being yanked so abruptly out of school meant that graduating with her class was now unlikely unless she could get back soon to her studies. This close—she wanted to finish.

There were only two things that bothered her more than missing those classes and the ensuing graduation. The first was that two weeks had passed and there was no word from, or appearance by, Reece. She reasoned that he was a busy man and might have to tie up some loose ends and make some arrangements before leaving his business. She knew too that he was more a doer than a sayer so he might show up unannounced. But, secondly, it could also mean he had simply written her off and now would fill the vacancy with someone else. 'Not right away though,' she thought, 'he is such a careful planner that, unless he was recruiting two of us at the same time, it will take him months to find a replacement. Long before that can happen I will be back knocking on his door—at some disadvantage perhaps but that can be overcome.'

Outside, her father had gathered a few tools and a coil of rope which he put in the car. He stood at the driver's door staring at the house for a moment but his anger and courage were both fading so he climbed into the Studebaker and drove away.

Amy washed the dishes then went back to bed and slept her way into dreams of a lush apartment with a big soft bed in which, for the first time in her life, she might not feel so utterly alone. And of rushing wet pavement seen by headlights over the long black engine cover of a long black car.

With the Coast mountains behind but still hundreds of miles to go that same long black McLaughlin rolled it's tall, wood spoke wheels like a summer storm across the semi desert of central Washington State.

Chapter 8

It was mid afternoon when Ruff drove by his home with the first load of lumber tied precariously onto poles that were in turn tied to the front and rear bumpers and left sticking out wide enough to pile the boards onto. The Studebaker's springs were too light to carry many at a time so it was going to take two trips. It also meant climbing in the open window after the lumber was piled along the side since it made the doors impossible to open.

He expected the kid to be gone by the time he returned to Dolph's Camp for the second load but the first thing he saw as he rounded the last corner of the draw leading down to the place was little Buck nibbling his way along near the water. The buckskin watched his approach for only a moment then beat him up the last short climb to the level of the bench where the remains of the buildings stood. Like a faithful dog he went to the recumbent form of his partner in crime and stood guard as Ruff drove to the pile of boards.

'That stupid horse doesn't trust me,' Ruff mused. He wished the kid had gone. After the shooting contest—at least that's what he had intended it to be—had turned into a rout they had both been stiff and uncomfortable. Ruff in shock from what he had witnessed and ashamed of himself for forcing Eddy into the corner that had made him so desperate as to try such an impossible shot. It had to have been luck, and tons of it, that guided the bullet to the raven but Ruff's pride in his own shooting, one of the very few things he considered himself to be a master of, was now—at least for the moment—as completely destroyed as the raven was. Oddly, Eddy too seemed to be ashamed of that good shot but for him it was more the shame of having shamed the older man. They had loaded the car in near complete silence agreeing on how to do it with hardly a word between them.

"Took you long enough."

"My tires aren't very good—I took it pretty slow."

"You did too. Man could die of heat inhalation or even plain old starvation while waiting here. I can think of better places to donate my carcass to."

"You didn't have to wait for me."

"I did too. I'm generally pretty careful I don't get anything heavy duty started but when I do make that mistake, I like to see it through."

'Well,' Ruff thought, 'this testiness is probably an improvement over the silent shame that lay between us two hours ago.'

"There you go." As he tied the last knot holding the last of the boards to the side of the car Eddy stepped back and brushed his hands together as if finally rid of some thoroughly distasteful chore.

"You want to go ahead? I make a lot of dust in places."

"No. Go on. By the time I get Buck saddled it won't be too bad. I'll only follow a little ways anyhow then I'll turn off and make a run for home A-fore I plumb fall apart of malnutrition."

"A-fore?"

"Yup. Comes ahead of B-fore and that's got me scared. Gonna have to make some fast tracks home to get there A-head of it or my tummy will start thinking there's been a B-head job done. Reb will have the cure spread out on the table in jig time."

"Reb? Oh yes, your mother. Okay then—." Ruff stopped himself just in time before saying, 'see you tomorrow' because he expected Eddy's help had now come to an end.

Ruff stopped at home with this second load, crawled awkwardly out the window and went in to see if Amy had supper ready.

"How was I to know when you would be back? You and Eddy vanish into the dust like a pair of vagabonds without a word of your intentions. What am I supposed to do—cook up a meal then watch it spoil while waiting for you?"

"No, Amy, it's okay. I'll go unload this lumber then I'll be back in about an hour—will that be better?"

"Not a bit! That will make us too late. I want to take a walk yet this evening. Sit down and I'll have it ready in ten minutes but it will be cold. If you think I'm going to light a fire in this heat then you can think again."

'Ah, Amy, you have learned well. Too well!'

After eating, Ruff drove on to the site of his flume to unload the lumber. Mr. Simon, owner of the sawmill, was standing there with hands on hips looking over the preparations. "So you're going to block off my road here by crossing it with a flume are you?"

"Well," Ruff groped for some understanding of the disapproval in Simon's voice, "actually I didn't think of this as a road. I thought you were all done logging everything that would come in this way."

"Hard to say. I might put a road up the sidehill and haul through here from the flat above. Lots of wood up there yet to come in."

"But, I thought you would haul it along on top then down your main road from the northeast. Comes in better to the log dump that way."

"Hard to say. I just might bring it this way if it turns out to be shorter."

"Pretty soft ground here though compared to where your main road is." This time Ruff pointed west to the road he had driven in on which was also the main haul road for logs coming in from all points south as well as lumber going out to the railroad. It was less than a hundred yards on over.

"It's all hard in the winter."

"Yes, I guess it is." In the winter Ruff wouldn't care if he was getting water or not. The little stream in his ditch would probably freeze solid anyway. "I could make this centre section so it could be removed easily for when you want to haul through here."

Simon frowned, "that might help some. I might not have to tell my crew to tear the whole thing down."

Ruff shuddered at the thought. "I'll make sure the centre is easy to lift out and if you let me know ahead of time I'll do it for you. That way it won't cost you a cent."

"Hmf," Simon's snort was neither approval nor disapproval but actually more like he was thinking up some further objection. "Where did you get that lumber?"

'Could that be it? He's angry simply because I didn't buy my lumber from him? Such a piddly little amount to him who has entire truck loads going out every day—it shouldn't matter.'

Ruff told him.

"Say Ruff, I wouldn't get mixed up in that if I were you. That place still belongs to Dolph. You might find yourself in court over those boards—maybe even in jail."

"Uh. But it's such a small amount and everyone else in the country has been there ahead of me so there is hardly anything left of the buildings already."

"Hard to say, probably just means you will have lots of company when they come tracking it down. Not hard to see it doesn't come from my mill—too old and already has nail holes in it— won't take them long to find it."

'Not if you tell them where to look,' Ruff thought. "Eddy seemed to think Dolphs' are gone from here and not likely to ever be back."

"Ah. I should have seen Eddy's work in this. He's good to have on your side, Ruff, he can fix about anything that runs but you better keep him on a short rein because he tends to swing a wide loop now and then." For the first time Simon's mouth showed the faintest smile. "Your car running pretty good now?"

'Oh, no! He knows.' Right now is the moment to apologise and offer to pay for the points that Eddy has switched. But how does one offer to pay for something that is probably worth close to a dollar when buying those chocolate bars with cash instead of charging them has left exactly six cents in one's pocket! His face flamed red, giving him away but since he didn't know how to make a joke of it he missed the opportunity.

"Yes, it runs okay." How he wanted to add, 'since Eddy worked on it,' and shift the blame to where it belonged.

"Hmf, thought it might be giving you ignition troubles like mine is."

"No. No, it's not."

'And now the chance is past! Now the blame lies right here. The very best I can do now is to pretend ignorance of the whole thing.'

There was no longer any hint of amusement on Simon's face as he turned to go back toward the houses but even his parting shot could sink Ruff no lower.

"Hard to say about you putting that ditch along the hill above the houses. If it breaks over it's banks that whole stream could be in somebody's back door and it better not be mine!"

Ruff, a painfully honest man, unloaded his stolen boards, his stolen nails and spikes, climbed into his stolen car and still running on the undoubtedly stolen gasoline that Eddy had poured in, drove home. True, only the points—such a small though vital part—were stolen. Or swapped? No! Stolen is the correct word because the rightful owner knew nothing of the exchange.

Nothing, that is, beyond suspicions formed from remembering how badly Ruff's car had run two weeks ago and hearing it run so good today along with finding his own car now running poorly! And he probably knows that Eddy is calling on Amy.

Amy was not at home when he got there and that suited him just fine because he did not want to have to find some way to talk with her now. At supper he had put off saying anything about the way she had acted at breakfast and he knew now that he never would hold her to task for it. That need to clear the air would just lie inside him—a growing, festering soreness along with so many other things with whom there was no one to talk it over with. Certainly not Corrie with her frivolous, not-long-out-of-school, young girl mind who wasn't here anyway and couldn't help him if she was. He had already made her either angry or · embarrassed, dozens of times by talking without thinking as he could have done with Libby—as Libby so often did with him.

Amy was really only one of many worries and while perhaps she was now the most obvious and immediately pressing she was definitely not the biggest—or even near the biggest. He refused to count the years he had been trying to make a farm of this waterless place. His contract with the Government would soon be up and if he had no crop of some sort growing they might not grant him the deed of ownership. So far he had lived up to their requirements by clearing away some trees to gain the appearance of a squared up field. There hadn't been many to cut down since most of what he planned to work into a field had been a natural prairie amidst the timber. With his wheelbarrow he had trundled tons of rocks from this 'field to be' and heaped them up in piles along it's edge. He looked with pride on those piles of rocks and wished for cement so he could build a stone fence around the place. In one corner of low ground where the soil was good and moisture gathered until the deep dry of summer he had grown a garden and had built this house and a root cellar. But unless there could be some sort of a major crop this year he could lose it all.

There—his mind had counted the years since filing papers on the place without his consent.

Even just the wild grass, teased by adding water into looking like hay ready to cut, should be enough. For that to happen the ditch must be working within days now—not months or even weeks. With this heat wave it would soon be too late to save the grass for this year for it would burn dry right down into it's roots and wouldn't by any stretch of the imagination look like a crop of hay. Might even be gone until next spring. Just the flume to build now and a short bit of connecting ditch to dig. He tried to count it up in days to completion but this time his mind refused to let him have the answer and veered off on a tangent instead.

'Rain! What I need most is a week of heavy rain. It would also soften the ground for digging.'

He felt the crush of his own past history closing in on him too. How many times before this had success almost been within his grasp only to elude him at the last instant? He had never been able to work for someone else for very long at any one time so his entire life story was made up of misguided ventures that had failed—often through no fault of his own. If this one too were to fail now, so close to the finish line, then he may never try again. He did not explore that thought any further. Would not!

'Marriage too is a venture,' he mused. 'I have let one fail—I must hold on to this one even though it may not have been wise to get into it in the first place.'

Why had it even happened? Through working for Simon and eating at the cookhouse after Libby left he had come to know Corrie—only slightly at first—as the latest in a succession of cooks come to work at the sawmill camp. Then, stung by the sudden ending of a romance of her own, she had ambushed him and thereby supplied Libby with ammunition for the divorce. Or had he ambushed her while she was vulnerable?

Maybe they had ambushed each other.

He needed her here now. He needed someone to talk to—someone other than Amy! The car ran good now—he could drive her to work every day again. She didn't like Amy but they had never met so how could she know for sure—they might actually get along quite well together—not much age difference.

'I should've gone to the cookhouse to visit while I was up there tonight. It's not too late yet and there's enough gasoline in the car for one more trip to the mill. I'll worry about gasoline tomorrow.'

Within minutes and without thinking about Corrie's need to be up before dawn, he was on his way back up the road for the third time in one day.

At the cookhouse he found the door locked so, not overly surprised, he went around to the back entrance but it was locked too. He knocked loudly on the door. Thirty seconds later he pounded harder and this time he heard movement inside that sounded like the door to the sleeping quarters being opened. He had one moment for doubt before Corrie unlocked the door and pulled it back just enough to see who it was.

"It's late, Tru, have you no sense of time? I have to be up in the morning you know." She wore a housecoat and held it closed at the neck with one hand while the other held the door from opening wider. She looked heat frazzled and flushed.

"I have to talk to you Cor, let me in." He pushed on the door, almost getting in but she surged against the other side with surprising force shoving him back down the step. The lock clicked as he reached for the knob and short of smashing down the door he was locked out.

"Go away, Ruff," was all he heard from inside. Instead, he stood there in shock and disbelief—not at being told to leave but at what had been so painfully obvious as his one step inside had let him see through the open door into Corrie's private room. On the floor—folded neatly just as if they rested there every night— a pair of tan trousers and in the same short instant a man's hand snatching them out of sight and pulling them away to where the bed would be.

Without being aware of moving he found himself in the Studebaker with his hand on the ignition switch and his foot against the starter pedal but not actuating either one. There was just one thought in his mind. "Who is it?"

Around him the camp was quiet. The only movement in sight as dusk settled was three boys playing at his water ditch not far from Simon's house. Sailing boats? There was probably enough water in the ditch to do that as it trickled along and spilled out the unfinished end. He couldn't care less as long as they didn't break the bank down. That image of normal activity brought him back to his senses to the point where he remembered something the kid had once said. "- when I look at him I think of coyote—opportunist—and I never would trust a coyote around my hen house—not even a tame one."

"That gives me an idea who. That dumb kid see's too much!" He started the car and drove to the little building that served as commissary, post office and living quarters for the time keeper. 'If Errol is home then I am wrong but if the place is closed and locked—.'

But the store was open, so, since he had parked in front of it and gone to the door he went on in. Inside, however, he found it was the younger brother, Floyd, who was in charge tonight. He looked more than a little flustered to see Ruff.

"Evening, Mister Ruff. What's going on tonight that brings you out?"

"I—ah—I need some gasoline, Floyd. If you have a drum up on the rack I'd like to fill the tank on my car."

"Sure thing, I can sell you some gas but only if you pay in cash."

"What's that? I've a charge account here. Errol always writes it down for me. Where is Errol anyway?"

"Oh, he had to go out tonight and I sure hate to be the one who has to tell you this but he warned me specifically that you've been put on a cash only basis."

"But—but I've always been able to charge here. Why not now?" 'Could Simon be so angry that he is meddling and making trouble for me?'

"I'm sorry Mister Ruff but your wife served notice both here and to Simon that she won't pay your bill any more."

The young man was sweating and plainly very uncomfortable. 'I would be too,' Ruff thought, 'if I had to tell a man something like this. And, besides that, he knows very well where his brother is. Just as I know altogether too well where his brother is—I've seen those tan pants before.'

"I'm terribly sorry but if I sell anything to you on credit, it will come out of my own wages."

"No, that's okay Floyd, I understand. I didn't bring any money with me tonight so I'll come back another time. Good night."

"Good night, Mister Ruff."

Outside he started the car and drove away from the store but stopped where he could see the cookhouse. 'If I were a real man I would take my rifle, smash down the door and shoot them both. That's what a real man is expected to do isn't it? I guess I am not a real man because I couldn't end their lives over such a—. No! It's not a trivial thing. It's a monstrous act they have done to me but still, I cannot end lives over it. It would be the end of mine too.'

He sat there, engine running, gasoline level in the tank dropping lower as shadows around him darkened—night moving in for the kill—crawling over the fatally injured but still writhing body of the day barely past. He moved the headlight control to 'on' and the beams seemed to light the way for him in more ways than one. He pressed the clutch, pulled the shifter into gear and followed the bright lights as they lifted or dipped with the road leading him toward home.

The fatalistic bent in his mind now worked to save him for he was already thinking in the past tense when he thought of Corrie—she was gone—more thoroughly gone even than Libby was gone. But at the same time it poisoned his mind toward himself for he worried now about what he had done wrong to cause this and what he might have done right to keep it from happening. Was he even capable of doing anything right? He knew that he would feel the hurt more next week than he did now and more yet next month but for tonight he would manage—after all—if there was any one role into which he fitted well it was as a survivor. Beaten up and bent but never broken. He would survive this too.

The car sputtered and jerked then caught again. Almost home. He swung off the main road onto his own two ruts keeping the engine running by pulling the choke on each time it faltered. The Studebaker rolled to a dead engine stop only ten feet short of it's proper parking place.

Less than a hundred miles away the black McLaughlin stopped high on a rock bluff looking over Moyie Lake. The gleam of water was barely discernible down below in the darkness. Inside, the driver turned on an overhead light and for the third time since crossing back into Canada at Kingsgate, studied his map.

'Has to be the right route—not much of a road—shows a big lake about here alright.' His thoughts went slowly on, struggling through the tiredness that did little to improve his frame of mind, 'I can't believe I've come this far—farther even than I thought it was but there's too much investment involved here to write her off so easily—in time if not in money. That girl has got a debt to pay and I'm just the fellow to collect. I'll drive in and have a good laugh at her being cooped up all alone on that little homestead of her father's—a perfect place for her—then I'll leave her there to sweat it out until she comes to realise that she's nothing special.'

Less than an hour later the chromed falcon perched on the radiator cowl with wings spread to catch the updraft flowing from the road surface ducked under the stone and wood arch that welcomed him to Cranbrook. With over forty hours and hundreds of miles passed since he last climbed out of bed Reece cruised the short main street, chose the best looking hotel and took their most expensive room where he folded for the night.

Chapter 9

The house was dark at every window so Amy was either not at home or she had gone to bed and this early at night that would be worthy of recording. After lighting the gas lamp Ruff went near the doorway to her room and called but there was no answer. Since the door was open he carried the lamp inside to look around. What he was expecting he would not have put into words but the image of empty drawers and missing suitcases were in his mind until he saw that everything was in place.

He went outside wondering what to do. She must be lost! In a way he hoped she was lost because the alternative seemed too obvious—that she was not alone.

Now, with no bright headlamp beams in front of him the night was not as dark as it had seemed when he had driven in and walked from the car into an unlit and empty house. There was a sliver of moon and a lot of starlight and it had finally cooled to an almost comfortable level—a night for lovers. Has her 'gangster' arrived? No word from Libby about that yet but he could think of no other reason for her to stay out so late. He moved away from the house, beyond the hissing noise of the gas lamp coming from each open window and with hands cupped to ears listened in every direction in case she was calling for him. It was so still that he would have heard her from a mile away but there was nothing except the trill of a nighthawk every few seconds. There must be dozens of them diving then pulling out with a whirring boom of wing feathers.

Perhaps he should call for her? Perhaps walk the back roads calling?

No!

He was afraid to in case she did not want to be called for—did not want to be found. Instead, he went into the house and pumped up the gas lamp more so it would stay bright longer and left it on the table to shine out the windows as a beacon then carried a chair outside. He settled it under the nearest big pine tree and prepared himself to wait and listen for as long as it took.

Half an hour later it occurred to him that if she has to wander lost all night it might do her more good than harm—she might stay closer to home in the future. Once daylight comes so the mountains can be seen she will not remain lost for she grew up here and knows her way around as well as anyone. Certainly the weather is not a factor to worry about—as long as she keeps moving she won't even feel a chill. He worried anyway.

He worried more yet after the Rum Runners made their presence known. Three cars travelling slowly and spaced out enough to let some dust settle from the one ahead. Quiet engines in silent cars—in daytime they might have gone by unnoticed except for their dust. Now the air was so still that since he was already sitting outside and listening hard for any small sounds he heard their murmur a mile coming and expected to hear them a mile going. Ordinarily they would not have awakened him from even a light sleep. He hoped Amy was nowhere near the road or had enough sense to hide if she was.

He sat up straight when the lead car slowed and turned in on his road. He stood up, thoroughly alarmed, when the second car also slowed for the turn. When the third car followed the first two he slipped behind the tree to avoid the headlights swinging his way. One after the other they all stopped at the house.

After a minute or two that felt like an hour to Ruff, the driver of the lead car got out and went swiftly with long strides to the open kitchen door.

"Anybody home?" He called it loudly then with no hesitation entered the building. The other two drivers also climbed out of their vehicles but stayed away from the light coming from the windows of the house as well as that from their own headlamps. Ruff caught the gleam of guns in the hands of the second two. More astonished than frightened he would have slipped away into the forest except for the sudden thought that Amy could walk innocently into this scene at any moment. The man who had gone inside now came out in a rush at the same time pulling something metallic from a pocket. It reflected light from the gas lamp until he stepped into the shadows.

"There's nobody here—it could be a trap!"

None of them made any movement while they thought this over for a few seconds then a calmer voice said, "I don't think so. We know where everybody is tonight and Eddy says this guy is okay." After another moment for thought the same voice called out, "Mr. Ruff, are you nearby?"

Still more afraid for Amy than for himself and with the sure knowledge that he had committed no crime so could walk with the safety of an honest man, Ruff came from behind his tree. His steps faltered when he remembered Eddy—and the stolen car repairs—and the stolen lumber and nails. But it was too late now for they had heard him and three bright beams of light converged on his face. He mentally heaved a great sigh of relief— not guns—flashlights.

"What are you doing out there?" The voice was authoritative but not threatening. It was also somewhat familiar.

"It's too hot in the house. I've been sitting out here watching the stars, listening to the nighthawks and enjoying the night air." Ruff was surprised at the friendly tone he managed. Reason told him these men were liquor smugglers—he knew from the voice that he was going to recognise one of them and that might not be good. The mention of Eddy—he may have heard wrong—he hoped he had heard wrong.

"Ah, that sounds very sensible and enjoyable. I wish we had time to join you but we have come to pick up our freight from your root cellar and then we must be on our way." Without waiting for a reply from Ruff he addressed his companions, "You can go over and load up while I keep Mr. Ruff company. Since we are both trying to make a living from a dry farm we have a lot in common." Two flashlights were immediately turned off and the third turned downward as though to assist Ruff as he picked up his chair and walked to the house. "Is your daughter with you?"

"No, she's not home. She's out—visiting."

"Ah well, nice to be young and fancy free."

The two other drivers both climbed into the lead car and obviously knowing the way, drove to Ruff's root cellar. After they turned off the car lights they became quite invisible except for the occasional glimpse of a flashlight beam. Ruff's companion went to both cars by the house and turned all the lights off but left the engines idling.

Ruff placed his chair on the porch and made himself comfortable but—typically—didn't think to offer to get a chair for his 'guest' who sat himself down on the edge of the porch floor where he was not in the lamp light from either the door or the window. He asked a few questions about the progress of the ditch and Ruff found easy answers.

"Unfortunately, my place is so high on a dry hill that there is very little possibility that I will ever get water to it. Not unless I can raise the money to buy more than a mile of quite large steel pipe and enough more to have it installed. I've tried digging a well but with no luck."

Ruff knew for sure now who he was talking to but did not try too hard to remember the name preferring instead to give the impression that—even if he did know—he had no intention of ever mentioning tonight's visit to anyone.

The man in the shadows carried ninety percent of the conversation explaining how he had adjusted his plans to work around the lack of water by using his property as little more than a home base to live on while earning his living at other ventures. Despite the worrisome strangeness of the visit Ruff found himself interested in the man's story and was actually disappointed when the others came back to report that they "had it all" and were ready to go.

"Then we are on our way," the man on the porch announced. He pulled an envelope from a vest pocket and handed it to Ruff. "A token of appreciation for your help Mr. Ruff. We were surely in a bad fix with a car breaking down on us and no safe place to hide the freight while it made an empty run back for repairs. Thankfully, Eddy came along and suggested putting it in the root cellar. He wouldn't take any pay for his work on the car because he said his fix might not last long so you can tell him it took us safely all the way to the garage in town. And thank your daughter once again for the much appreciated refreshments she found for us. Between the two of them they quite literally saved the day for us. Good night Mr. Ruff. And good luck with the water ditch."

Ruff sat still for long enough that the three cars passed out of hearing to the south. "Well, I can sure use some good luck on the ditch but I did not need the rest of that." He had no trouble imagining what had happened. The Rum Runners must have been on the road with an ailing car while Eddy was coming to visit Amy. A daytime run—he knew that was common enough. "But Amy has lied to me. By omission only but just the same she has lied—again." Worse yet, he knew he would let her get away with it—again. It was better than—or rather—it was easier than confronting her with facts. As he stood to go in to pump up the lamp once more he realised he was still holding the envelope. It wasn't sealed so he lifted the flap and pulled out the contents.

Five ten dollar bills!

More than his take home pay would be for two months of working for Simon! He looked wildly about the room for a place to hide them but could not immediately think of a place Amy would not touch on as she went about her house work. He shoved them back into the envelope and stuffed it inside his shirt. All he knew for sure was that he could not keep it—it was not honestly earned money. Nor, he knew, could he give it back—it was not possible—the man would not want to be approached for that to happen.

He guessed that Eddy had lied by omission too but somehow that was different—to be expected—for Eddy it was entirely in character to help anyone having difficulty. He would have helped the Police with the same zeal. It was entirely in character for him to refuse payment too. And it was also quite in line for him to place so little importance on the matter that he might neglect to mention it later. 'But he should have told me so I could expect them. He must have thought they would come in daylight again while I was away working.'

'And what would I have done if I had known they were coming? I would probably have stewed over the right and the wrong of it until I talked myself into sending word to the police. I might have sent Amy to Simon's camp for safety then I might have smashed those bottles of booze and lain in wait with my rifle at the ready.'

"I guess it's a good thing Eddy didn't tell me."

'Who would have believed a Rum Runner could be such a normal, nice person? And another dryland farmer at that! One who has had the good sense to give up on it. I'd have messed it up good just as I've messed up everything else.'

After pumping up the lamp again he carried his chair back to the tree outside in the darkness and continued his vigil. Within ten minutes he was more worried for Amy's safety than angry at her for collaborating with the Rum Runners. But then an un-wanted thought came forward. 'On top of everything else—I—a lifetime tea-totaller and an honest law abiding citizen—am now a smuggler of liquor! I have stepped so far outside the law that I am now a serious criminal.' His head—and his spirits too—sank even lower.

It was well after midnight when he sensed that Amy was coming though he neither saw nor heard her until she was quite close. By then he had recovered some small bit of composure and her safe arrival cheered him. When he rose to greet her she jumped aside then laughed shakily with one hand to her throat. "Father! You startled me. I thought you would be asleep long ago. I'm afraid I let my mind wander off elsewhere so when you stood up so suddenly I thought something had me."

"I too was beginning to fear that something had you—the country is full of bears and cougars you know." But his thoughts actually ran more toward a certain gangster. Or passing rum runners to whom the McLaughlin seems to be the car of choice—big and heavy, fast and powerful. There was even a nickname relating the car to the illicit liquor trade but for the moment Ruff couldn't remember what it was. Something about rum and the size of the engine. No—not rum—whiskey. They were known as Whiskey Sixes. Just to own one brings on the winks and nods—if he drives a McLaughlin then he is up to no good.

"Oh, pooh. No bear or cougar will ever harm me. I'd be much more afraid if I happened across some people out there."

"You might be right, obviously you have no fear and any animal would sense that and perhaps leave you alone. Perhaps! On the other hand, they do get hungry you know. Unlike you, I am afraid of them. I've not always been but over the years I've had too many close calls and questionable encounters to be otherwise. I think they sense that defensive fear so now I am only safe when I have my gun."

"Well, I don't need a gun. I wouldn't shoot any animal even if I had one."

"Just because I carry the gun doesn't mean I am going to shoot anything—it just means I can if I have to. It means I can make a lot of loud, threatening noise and usually that's all that's needed."

She didn't answer that but once inside the kitchen she surprised him by asking if he would like a cup of coffee.

"Yes, I would, very much at that." Then, remembering the nearly empty coffee can, "actually, no. I think I'd prefer a cup of tea," and gave away his reasoning, "we've lots of that."

Amy laid a fire of pitch pine shavings and dry fir bark chips, left the stove lid off and set the kettle over the open flames. It was singing hot in no time at all though the kettle took on some smoke blackening in the process.

'She has not forgotten how to do it—she has fitted in here as if she has never been away.'

"Are we broke?"

"I'm afraid so." He had already forgotten the unwanted fifty dollars inside his shirt.

"And out of credit?"

"Yes."

Neither of them spoke for several minutes.

"And I have no money to help out with either." There was no way she would dip into her train ticket reserve for anything.

"It's alright, we'll get by."

"Well, at least we have potatoes, carrots and turnips in the root cellar and most of the basics in the pantry so we won't starve but there won't be many luxuries."

"No." Mention of the root cellar sent him into a downward spiral again.

They sat in what she thought a comfortable silence but her father felt as the weight of a strained silence until the tea was all gone and still they sat beyond that. Even the tiny fire to boil the kettle had added more heat to the room but neither of them seemed to care. It was still cooler than daytime had been.

At least it was out in the open now—he didn't have to pretend to her that he hadn't been living on his wife's income. Nor that he wasn't allowed to anymore.

"Did she leave because of me?"

Ruff took his time answering because until tonight he would have thought the answer to that question must be 'yes' but now he knew that Amy's arrival had only been the final straw. More excuse than reason. Though he hadn't seen it coming he knew now that Corrie had been lost to him long before Amy came to stay and she would have left soon anyway.

"No, you can put your mind to rest on that, she merely tired of this place and of me too. I should have known it sooner but I was so busy that I didn't."

"Mom came to hate it too, it's why she left."

'Your mother left because I let her think the farm was more important to me than she was. She left to teach me a lesson that I wasn't smart enough to learn. I should have gone with her but once she ran off to the Coast I was too stiff necked to follow.' "I suppose you hate it here too."

"Why no," she surprised even herself with the intensity of her answer, "this is my home—it's where I come from. It has been so lonely here but even so it will always be the secret place I can close my eyes and go to when I need it. I love to walk the ridge behind and to the lakes too—all of them—especially at evening and into the night. Eddy says one of those lakes is named after you—why is that?"

"Oh, it's just a little pothole of a lake—like me—not too significant in any way. It's named after me because I tried to raise the money to siphon water out of it and over the ridge to here. Turned out the lake is probably too low in elevation relative to the field to make it work."

"Oh."

"Yes"—'another failure.'

"There are things about being here that I don't like of course. I don't much care for this dingy little house—"

'Of my design and construction—I couldn't afford anything better. So hard to work out for money and to work at home too.'

"—and I don't care for the isolation or the dust and hot sun of summer and the cold snow and ice of winter. I've been at the Coast long enough now to see rain as much easier to live with. You would do well to move out there too—it's a much better place to farm than here. But I guess most of all I've been ashamed of the poverty that we have always tried to deny."

Ruff cringed and thought he kept it inside but it must have shown.

"I'm sorry Father but it had to be said. You are always working so hard at something that perhaps you don't notice or just don't care how people look at us. But I care. And Mom cares too. Sometimes it is so hard to keep one's head up and meet the neighbours stares eye to eye but Mom has taught me that it must be done."

"Do you—that is—are you still short of money? Out there too? I thought your mother had a job."

"She does. But it pays so little and she has kept me in school so I haven't been much help to her. I hope to change that soon because I am nearly done with school no matter that she may want me to go farther with it. It's a good thing Aunt Helen has seen fit to be generous once in a while."

Ruff looked up at the change in tone and caught the sarcastic sneer on her young face. He looked down again.

"Good night Father."

This time he was slow looking up so that when he did she was already gone. He sat up straighter but then leaned forward to lay his head on his arms on the table top. He was near the bitter end of his rope. Again! He knew that no amount of squirming would find a way out of this mess. He had been here before and he recognized all the signs and symptoms only now he has dragged Amy into it as well. Now she will witness the final falling apart of all those years of striving and sacrifice. Maybe it would be best if her 'gangster' came quickly and rescued her from it. But would it be rescue or something worse?

He wished once again that he had been able to swallow his stubborn pride and go west after Libby. Any place would be better than here if his family was with him.

"No! I have to finish what I've started." He sat up and raised an arm, fist clenched, to bang it on the table but slowed it's descent so that it landed soundlessly.

He stared at that fist on the table in front of him with some incredulity. A slow and faint smile twitched his mouth—a victory of sorts—two of them in fact! He had brought his temper under control almost as quickly as it had flamed—and he had smiled. As long as a man can find something to smile about there must be hope. He went to his room and flopped face down on the bed with all his clothes on and his boots too.

In Cranbrook, just sixty miles to the west, the McLaughlin's owner slept the dreamless reward of the very tired.

At Hope, hundreds of miles to the west, the daily Kettle Valley Branch Line passenger train left the main Canadian Pacific tracks along the Fraser River to turn up the Coquihalla Valley. On one single straight stretch drilled into the Coquihalla Canyon the track threaded five tunnels and two river crossings and wasn't even an overly long straightaway. From there the train climbed on toward places with the strangest names—Othello—Lear—Iago—Romeo—and Juliet. The Supervisor of construction had been a fan of Shakespeare.

In the first coach behind the mail and baggage cars where her bench seat would have to serve to sleep on through two nights and the day between, sat Mrs. Libby Ruff. She watched the convoluted scene outside fade into the coming night and wished mightily for full daylight by which to assess the danger—or complete darkness to hide the shadowy crags and crevices through which the train crept and creaked it's slow way.

"Close your eyes," a voice in the back of her mind said. The voice sounded suspiciously like Amy who in turn sounded eerily like Libby's sister Helen who had grudgingly supplied the funds for this 'reckless extravaganza'.

"I most certainly will not!"

Chapter 10

"You're late! What's the matter, can't get up in the morning?"

"More like I couldn't get to bed last night," Ruff grumbled.

He had almost not come to the flume site at all this morning. Rising as early as ever despite his late night, he had sat longer than usual over his slowly eaten, solitary breakfast. In vain he had tried to form some plan that would get him going in some positive direction again. His talk with Amy last night—or to be more accurate—Amy's talk with him had sunk him into depths of despair far below what his encounters with Simon and later with Corrie had done. That his daughter must now see him as such a bumbling, useless, perennial loser struck him right to the heart. She hadn't said it quite so bluntly—hadn't used those words and might not have known how well they fit but intentional or not, she had driven home the message from which he now picked out his own meaning.

He worried on, 'that's probably the way my wife—wives—yes, both of them, came to see me. No wonder they left—they wanted something better.'

He looked around the room in which he sat. It really wasn't all that bad! No worse than what many others of the early settlers lived and thrived in so why was this place so different? 'It must be that they, Libby and Corrie—and Amy too, can't see the future of it. All they see is the drudgery and hardship of the present. Well, I'll show them yet!'

That surge of anger had carried him out of the house in such a rush that, for the first time since she had come, he left his dirty dishes for Amy to wash and didn't even realise that he had done so. By the time he walked half the distance to the flume site his burst of anger driven enthusiasm had waned, his steps slowed and his mind was back to beating at the walls of the corner in which he was trapped.

He needed money! That's it, plain, bald and simple. It seems nothing works smoothly without it. He could earn money by going to work in a lumber camp but then the farm would be lost because he would not be able to 'prove up' in time.

So he also needed to stay at home to work on the ditch to make the farm a practicality. But, if he did that, then there was no money to buy the things he needed just to keep eating and living, never mind to purchase the implements and seeds to grow and tend a crop. So the farm would be gone that way too and just as quickly only with more work put into it before it went.

And the tractor he had so blithely told the kid he was going to get! His steps slowed even more. If there were someone to buy the car, someone who could pay cash for it, then he could carry on a little longer. But it was older than it's years indicated having been driven with no maintenance on so much bad road. The tires all worn out and full of repairs that bumped with each revolution and the radiator leaked—it wasn't worth much—a small fraction of what he needed. If the car went then he would be afoot!

So what? He was afoot now unless he somehow raised the money for gasoline.

He smacked his forehead with an open palm—"circles, circles and more circles," he groaned aloud.

That's when he spotted Eddy at work and he stopped a moment to watch before walking on in. He was still lost and undecided but took the kid's rough greeting the way it was meant to be taken—with a grain of salt—and somehow it made him feel better.

"Don't just stand there gawking, man, get your grubhoe and bed in these sill chunks that Buck and I have dragged in so I can notch them for the uprights."

Ruff looked at the small green logs Eddy had laid in place, two for every length of the boards he had hauled in yesterday. "Shouldn't we peel them?"

"Yup. We should. But I thought you was in a hurry."

"I am but they'll rot away too quick left unpeeled."

"They will too. But if they do like fence posts do around here they'll rot away almost as quick even if we do peel them. What we really need is some pitch pine chunks but there ain't time to go looking for them unless it's next year you want the water."

"No, this'll do, I can always replace them another year."

"Sure you can."

"You sound as though you don't believe that will happen."

"Aw. I reckon if this here fakealoo works for you then it'll get rebuilt as needed."

"And if it doesn't then it won't—is what you are saying."

"Sure. Makes sense don't it? If it don't work you ain't about to waste the time. If it don't work quite good enough you might want to make it bigger. If you want to listen long enough I can think up a dozen different possibles for you."

"Point taken, Ed, point taken"

They worked through the morning with very little talk until they came to the centre section that crossed the barely perceptible tracks of an old, long unused truck road.

"Ah, Ed?"

"Yup?"

"Simon says we have to make this section of the water box removable in case he wants to haul logs through here."

The kid straightened without the board he had bent over to pick up. "When did he say that?"

"He was here last night when I brought in the last of the lumber."

"Huh. I wouldn't pay no attention to that nohow was I you, Ruff. He won't never haul logs through here again. Makes no sense."

"That's more or less what I said to him but he said he might build a road up the sidehill and haul through here from above."

"Naw. He might be stubborn but he sure ain't stupid. That'll never happen. Put it right out of your mind, Ruff."

"You're right about him not being stupid—he knows about the ignition points you -ah—put in my car."

"Sure he does. Why wouldn't he?"

"Well. How would he?"

"Oh. Easy enough. Cause I told him so is why. Just would have taken him a little while to figure out what I said is all."

"Just the same, he was not a happy man last night."

"Aw. Well. I reckon he's got lots to worry about what with this depression thing coming on. His markets ain't what they used to be and the prices are down and he sure ain't paying the wages he used to. Seems a man has to work for nothing and promise to pack in his own lunch to boot to get a job now days."

"He must pay you to cut and chop the fire wood or you wouldn't be so dedicated to it."

"Sure. He does too. But not so's you would notice. That's why he looks the other way when I eat at the cook shack and now and then pack off some little thing he don't really need as much as he thought he did. Speaking of—," Ed hauled a big stem winder of a watch from his pocket by the leather thong attached between it and a belt loop of his blue jeans. "Almost time now to go and help your wife and Floyd and Errol dispose of the leftovers. Didn't see you packing no lunch this morning—you coming too?"

"No!"

Seeing the tightened face, Ed changed the subject, "think I know what's bothering Simon."

"Oh?"

"Sure. His time here is numbered. He likely never gave it a thought back when he was setting up to start but now he can feel the end is getting to where he can see it's shadow. Unless price picks up for his lumber he won't be able to haul logs much farther than he already is doing now. Those old White trucks he uses to haul logs are about finished—the mechanic pretty well has to ride along on one or the other of them just to keep them running. What he needs is one or two like that big Leyland that hauls his lumber. That ain't likely to happen though cause they just plain cost too much for the way things are. So the day is coming when he will have to walk away from this place just like Dolph walked away from his. He might sell the mill machinery to somebody and the boiler room stuff and the trucks and maybe lots of the little things—cheap. But nobody is going to buy the buildings cause they weren't made to be moved. He can't stand the thought of us bush folk moving in and swiping the doors and windows then getting braver with time and tearing down everything for the boards and nails. Seeing that hint of what's to come to his camp, happening now to Dolph's, just plain makes him sick in his heart. Don't give him a second thought, Ruff, like as not he'll never come to look again and won't have another word to say."

Eddy pulled the watch out again for consultation. "And now that we have talked away half the morning I got to go build up my energy reserves or I won't be of no use at all to you this afternoon."

"That's quite a watch Ed," Too much watch for such a youngster to have. "Is that a gold case?"

"Aw. It is too. But. I reckon what you are really asking is—where did I get it?"

"Well—." Caught with his thoughts and suspicions on his sleeve, Ruff floundered.

95

"Fair question, Ruff, for sure I ain't worked enough years to earn half the price of a fancy trinket like this." Ed hauled out the watch again, slid it through the slotted end of the leather thong to release it from his pants and handed it to the older man.

Ruff held it one way then turned it over. "Waltham—nice engraving but no name or initials."

"Nope. My old father was real careful about things like that. He never kept anything that could be tracked. Found it among the things he never told me about nor where to look for until he knew his end was close. I reckon he stole it off some poor traveller he killed back in the mountains somewhere."

Ruff, shocked, dropped the big watch but Eddy caught it, deftly refastened it to his belt loop and slipped it into a pocket.

"Those are strong words, Ed. Does that mean all those stories about him are true? The killings and such?"

"Aw. I reckon. But likely less than half what he is given credit for 'cause he did like to take life easy now and then. He couldn't possibly have done more than half what some say he did."

"Ah, you never rode with him did you?" 'Whatever else, Amy, you sure can pick them. A gangster at the coast and a bandit here!'

"No, Ruff, I never. The only murder I am guilty of is of the spoken word. He was an old man crippled by arthritis long before I ever got to know him. I reckon he only took a wife when living got too hard for him to do it alone."

"So, he is dead now?"

"He is too."

"What did he die of?"

"You're thinking the hangman, Ruff, but it's not so. He died a good death—if you can see death as good—of old age."

"I see. But your mother is still alive?"

"Oh, sure. Old Reb's a sight younger than you are. And healthy enough to last a while too."

They were quiet long enough for it to begin feeling uncomfortable. "If that's all for now why I reckon I am off to the cook shack. Gettin' plumb hollow."

"Sure, Eddy, see you later." Then, with a second thought, "say, Ed, would you pick up my mail while you're over that way?"

"Sure thing, Ruff. I'll do that little chore."

While Eddy helped dispose of the leftovers at the cookshack and Ruff worked on with nothing to eat, Reece was buying gas in Elko for his Whiskey Six. Following directions given by the gas station attendant he left Elko on the route pointed out. A few miles later, after winding around some sand cuts and up a twisty hill, he stopped, got out Amy's map and studied it yet again. It was quite clearly done but of a very small area. The only hint as to it's general whereabouts was a notation—'Elko'—plus one arrow pointing west labelled 'to Cranbrook' and another to the east 'to Fernie'. From these marks at the top of the page ran a broken line downward to a squiggle that must represent a river. Below that was where the map became more detailed with a solid line which must be the main highway leading to a place called Spreading Pine.

"This map is not much good to me until I get across this river," he twisted the map about to read the fine printed words, "the Elk River." He looked at the ruts ahead, thought of the trail behind then turned around and drove back toward Elko watching to see if he had somehow missed his road. Back at the gas station and assured that he had gone the right way, he now saw that one of the buildings nearby was a restaurant. He parked in front of it and went inside. With a 'road' like that ahead of him it might be best to eat first.

While he ate he thought of the girl at the end of this long, rough trail. 'She has some nerve—drawing me out into the boon docks like this. I'll have a word or two for her that should set her thinking straight before I laugh and drive away alone.' He stopped chewing. 'Who do I think I am fooling? Why would I be here staring out a dirty window at a bleak grey mountain I have never seen before if she has not somehow become very special to me?' He resumed chewing and explored that new thought a bit farther. It was a logical one for if she were not 'special' she would not have caught his attention in the first place. He will gladly take her back with him as long as she can see it to be on his terms.

Despite this new understanding of the situation—or perhaps because of it—his mood deteriorated even farther as he prepared to head south on that dirt trail again.

Stopped at Midway Libby slept, taking up as much room as she and her open suitcase could. New passengers getting on tended to leave her to her space so she had not yet had to share the seat. She would awaken as soon as the train got up speed and began to sway.

Chapter 11

"Say. I'm sure glad I took my time eating. If I'd of known you'd do so well without me I'd of had another piece of pie."

Ruff chuckled, "yes it's going rather well alright. Did I get any mail?"

"Sure you did. But not enough to brag about." The kid handed over one letter. "Might be more later, Errol got called out halfway through mail sorting to patch up somebody at the mill."

Ruff looked it over then turned it to see if there was a return address on the back since there was none on the front. The postmark was so smeared that he wasn't sure but it seemed as though it said 'Elko' but he knew of no one in Elko who would write to him so it had to be some other very short place name. Rather than open it in front of Eddy he shoved it inside his shirt as he had done with Libby's letter the other day. "Should've been a Free Press today."

The kid shrugged.

Eddy worked another hour then, with the flume nearly completed, announced he was packing it in and going to call it a day. "I worked here quite a while before you showed up this morning, Ruff, so I am starting to feel like it's been a long day."

"Okay Eddy. Looks like I should finish the flume in an hour or so and then I'm going to turn some water into it."

"Good plan. It'll leak like a sieve until those dry boards soak up some moisture and swell shut on the cracks."

"You know, Eddy, if you'd told me we could build this thing in one day I'd have said you were dreaming."

Eddy grinned, "it did work out good didn't it but that ain't all Ruff. We'll get the rest of your ditch done tomorrow and you can play mud pies in the water all you like after that."

"Now don't make me call you a dreamer after all. There must be nearly two hundred yards to dig yet to make the connection. We'll not be doing that in any one day. Nor two or three of them neither I suspect."

"Aw. You wait and see. I'll bring the makings with me tomorrow only I'll be a little later than usual."

"Okay, I'll be here. If you happen to be going past my place would you let Amy know that if she's wanting to go for a walk again tonight I'll fix my own supper."

"Right. See you tomorrow."

The kid was hardly out of sight when a thought struck Ruff. "Now! Did I just tell him it was okay by me if he and Amy wanted to go for a walk?"

"No. I don't think so."

"But. I seem to be drawling out one word sentences to start each line of thought. And out loud to no one but myself like he often does." He shrugged it away, "doesn't matter, I'll get over it once he's not around any more."

Reassured, he got on with his work but his thoughts stayed with the kid. 'He is a strange sort—he set me up for that conversation about his father by flashing that gleaming big watch until I had to ask about it. He wanted me to have the story direct from him so there was no misunderstanding. Poor sucker, he still thinks he has a chance with Amy.

Reece was on the road again and past the place where his turn around tracks still showed that no other vehicle had crossed his tire marks since. The road became a little better and he actually began to enjoy it. His foul mood of recent days began slipping away as the challenge of driving this winding road quickened his pulse and soothed his mind. The railroad alongside looked fairly straight but the road was not—it wound from one corner into another and up and down too but at least it had become smoother. He was soon driving at a rate of speed probably never before seen on this poor excuse of a road. His father, who did not drive at all, had lectured endlessly against such dangerous speeding but had eventually given up, bought the McLaughlin and put the boy on the whiskey runs where his racetrack driving and daredevil antics could be useful and even profitable.

What a car—the Whiskey Six! It stuck to the road as if glued down as long as he kept the big tires off the loose gravel between the packed tracks. The overhead valve Buick engine throbbed out the power whenever he called on it for acceleration. Such a marvellous marriage—the McLaughlin car and the six cylinder Buick engine—meant for each other—just like him and Amy. Whether his sudden swing to cheerfulness came from the thrill of the road or from finally being on the last leg of his long journey Reece couldn't say and didn't care but having admitted finally that Amy was special to him he could now see one step farther. Except that he still visualised her whistling to his tune.

The road swung away to the east, climbing into some low hills while the railroad continued on southward. Thoroughly happy—thrilled in fact—he felt himself floating lightly over the rises and into the dips then pressed tight to the seat while bottoming out of them. He flew at high speed over the top of a rise flowing into a dip that turned out to be not a dip at all but rather a short steep down hill followed by a very short flat then—nothing! The McLaughlin was nearly airborne before he saw what was ahead. Much too close for comfort the road veered sharply—very sharply—to the left and dived down into a void!

Far away, beyond a gap made blurry by the sense of unexplained empty space, the opposite side of that void rose as a timbered hillside with the road visible here and there where it climbed to the top.

As the car's weight came down on it's wheels at last Reece hit the brake pedal, standing on it for all he was worth and as he slowed he pressed the clutch too and jammed into a lower gear. He slewed to a gravel flying stop with more room to spare than he had expected but right alongside a nearly new Model A Ford. The Ford faced the opposite way as if it had just climbed out of the void and now paused to catch it's breath. Off to one side the Model A's driver sat against a tree watching with great interest and some alarm. He now scrambled to his feet and came to peer between the cars to see if they had touched. They had not—not even close.

"Say, Lad, I'm sure glad you have good brakes."

"You and me both!" The man looked very little the older of the two but Reece, more exhilarated than frightened by his close call, kind of liked the 'Lad' and let it stand.

"I doubt yon guard rail was ever meant to stop anything so heavy as a car like yours."

Reece glanced at the so called guardrail protecting the edge of the drop off—a few untreated fence posts, rotted and leaning, joined by small and sagging, unpeeled bullpine rails. "No, definitely not, it's more like a hitching rail for horses than a guard rail."

Meanwhile, the other man was taking a longer and more speculative appraisal of the McLaughlin. "Where you headed in such a hurry? Across the Line?" Then he backed off a step plainly wishing he hadn't asked.

Reece, amused by the step back and enjoying the other's sudden discomfort ignored the question. "That's quite a hole in the ground—what's down there?"

"Yes, 'tis indeed quite a hole, that's the Elk River down there. It's okay though, the road is good enough but you best gear down to low and don't let it roll like you were doing as you came over yon rise."

"Yes, I'll be more careful. The Elk River is it? Maybe you can help me out. I don't know the roads down this way and all I have is a hand drawn map with few details until I cross that Elk River. Would you look at it and tell me if I am on the right road?

The Ford's driver came back more than the step he had taken backward and Reece smiled at the move liking that admission of at least a small eagerness for adventure. "I'm looking for a short cut to the Dorr Road—there is supposed to be a place called 'Spreading Pine' somewhere along it."

"Oh, sure," he came closer yet to peer at the map, "but if it's going to Dorr you are wanting then you should have taken the other road. The one that turns off a couple miles west of Elko and goes through Baynes Lake and Waldo. Lot better road than this—'course the Coppers practically never come this way." He wiped a hand across his mouth as though to rid himself of the foot in mouth problem he was having.

"Let's see now, yes, this seems to be pretty much accurate. This road goes to the Customs house at Roosville, but back up here," he ran a finger tip back toward the line representing the Elk River, "is the cross road you want. It goes right through the Spreading Pine and on down to this junction where, if you turn right, you come to Dorr. But you probably best turn left instead and go along here, past Edwards Lake, and go south on this road. It takes you to the Customs House on the railroad but you can turn off anywhere through here and with a car like this you can cross the Line just about anyplace between the river and the mountains."

This time the man merely looked resigned to his fate and Reece was tempted to ask if he wanted to come along for the ride. "How far from the top on the other side of this gorge to where I turn off to Spreading Pine?"

"Oh, not far, you'll pass one farm on the left just over there," he pointed straight across the gap, "then a little ways along there are two places close together and the next turn off to the right is the one you want."

"That looks simple enough. I'd best get on my way then before someone else comes along and finds me blocking the road."

"Not likely to be much traffic unless you have somebody following. They wouldn't likely catch up to you anyway but watch for my family on your way down the hill. They should be climbing this side by now."

"Well, in that case, maybe I better wait here. What are they driving, another Ford?"

"Oh no, they're walking, they should be well this side of the bridge by now."

"Walking! What on earth for?"

"Oh, you'll see, it's much too dangerous to load so heavily. I wouldn't want to kill us all in one smashup."

"Yes, I see. I'll be careful and watch for them. And thank you for the help."

"You're quite welcome. This prohibition stuff has brought out some stupid laws down there hasn't it?"

Reece grinned but didn't answer as he pulled his gearshift into low and slowly swung around the sharp corner that a few minutes ago he had briefly feared he was going to attempt straight across without benefit of wings.

The hill was steep alright and narrow too but there were a few places where two cars could probably pass if reasonable care were taken. It was nearly straight and he could see well on ahead so tiring of the slow pace, he shifted to second gear and let the big car out a little snubbing it with the brakes now and then. As he came to the first corner he slowed a bit and held well to the outside. It was a good thing he did for just around the corner he came upon the family of the man who waited at the top. Two boys and three girls—all grade school age—scrambling up the bank to safety. Their mother, in a long dress that went nearly to the road's surface and wearing a gauze festooned wide brimmed hat, stood as close to the inner edge as she could get while watching the kids climb in front of her.

Reece waved as he coasted past but the mother had her back to him—too proud to climb—stolidly awaiting her fate—to be killed or missed and spared. But the oldest girl and both boys were watching him go by and all waved in return—the biggest boy quite exuberantly in spite of his mother's eyes turning to him. Reece laughed his pleasure and with the bridge now in sight shifted to high and rolled faster until he had to brake for the turn onto the wooden structure where he shifted back to second.

The uphill side was steeper at first and rough enough to put him down to low gear for a little ways. It was more winding too with two corners cribbed with logs to hold the hillside back from the road. On such an upgrade he could stop on a dime if he should meet another car so he was soon back in second driving as fast as he could without leaving the road at the corners. He raced his engine to high R.P.M.s on the straighter stretches, tires throwing gravel. He could well imagine the headshakes of dismay and disapproval from both parents of the family on the other hillside. Born to be a show-off, his smile widened as he imagined the children excitedly pointing at the dust cloud rolling behind him. He wished the kids were in the car with him enjoying the ride over this canyon their father was afraid to share with them.

Somehow, the woman on the hill made him think of Amy, the way she stood straight and tall. Frightened perhaps, as Amy had been frightened the first time he picked her up but thinking that she kept it from showing. He hadn't seen this woman's eyes so he could only wonder if they too were bold and blue with a hint of wild. With five children the wild was probably under control and the bold grown to brave instead. Still, there was a similarity and he wondered if they were related or if, because he was getting so close, he was merely seeing things as he wanted to.

By now he positively loved this road and the risks that driving it fast presented. He knew that many would see him as a big kid with a dangerous big toy just as his father had and his mother still did but he didn't care. In fact, he liked to play up to the image of the big tough guy with a boyish yen for speed, danger, and fancy women.

From the very first moment he had caught sight of Amy amid her gaggle of school chums he suspected the era of the fancy women may be coming to an end. On making enquiries he had been dismayed to discover that she was only seventeen years old at the time and that had nearly ended it before it started. A seventeen year old was unthinkable! Yet he had found himself driving to that street at school out time just to see her again—even more frequently after the day they had locked eyes and each of them knew what the other wanted.

So she was poor! So what? He certainly wasn't.

He knew her well now. What she wanted was the security that his money could buy. What girl didn't? But no other had ever told him so with such open honesty. He had always admired people who stood up to be counted as she did no matter what their station in life. Like the man at the top of the hill waiting for his family because he thought it safer for them to walk. He had obviously been wary of Reece and the big car but hadn't let that get in the way of being interested, friendly and helpful.

From the very first time he had Amy out for a drive he had loved the way she responded to the fast car rides in rain soaked darkness as he showed her that not even the police could catch him. A shrinking violet she was not! She might be country dumb in many ways but she was truly a kindred spirit when it came to speed and excitement. Allowing herself to be shipped off to her father he recognised as part of a game she was going to play and his first impulse had been to resist and force her to come back on his terms or be gone from his life. Now, with today's admission that she was special to him, he finally understood why that resolve had lasted only until he received her very carefully worded letter along with the map. It had been easy to read between the lines that if he came for her she wanted more than the expensive apartment and big allowance. That if he didn't come for her then she may still take the apartment deal and live up to it. She would also take him for every penny she could and when he tired of her she would leave without being pushed.

His sole reason in going to her mother with the letter was to see for himself what the mother of such a girl might look like. He had not been disappointed but typically had overdone the heavy handed, spoiled playboy part though he had no regrets for just acting out what he wanted others to think he really was. He could play games too.

On flat land again he drove at a relatively slow pace as he passed the farms and kept a watch for his road to the right. He was beginning to understand that what he considered no more than two ruts in the wilderness were classed as a road out here so this time he found his place to turn away to the southwest.

As the train slowed for it's brief stop in Grand Forks Libby went into her—'I need all the room I've got'—act curling up as if asleep on one side of the double seat with her suitcase open on the other. As long as the train moved and there was light enough to see the shapes of the passing countryside she watched out the window as if determined to memorise it all. It was going to take a lot of hard work to pay back the borrowed money for her ticket and she wanted something positive from the exercise.

Travelling this route was not a totally new experience for her—she had done it in the opposite direction when, with twelve year old Amy in tow, she had run away from Ruff. Her mind had been churning too many dismal and fearful thoughts on that trip and her eyes had been too blurred too often for her to remember anything other than the mounting of miles between her and home. Between her and Tru.

There was both a sister and a brother with young cousins to Amy living within a few hours walking distance of her home on

Ruff's Prairie who would have taken her in for as long as she needed but while she wanted Ruff to come after her—she did not want it to be that easy for him. So the present troubles were as much her own fault as his because she had over done it by going too far—all the way to sister Helen's at the coast. He had misread her degree of determination (she should have known he would) and had not followed.

But another woman and divorce had.

When word came that he was about to marry that other woman she had made the trip alone because she had to go and see for herself if anything could be salvaged before it was too late even though the divorce had been her own impulsive reaction to hearing of Corrie. For some strange reason unmarried sister Helen had been unexpectedly understanding, encouraging and helpful on that one. It had been a disaster. Other than that it was in November and the entire return trip from Hope to Elko and back had been in a snow storm, or fog, or darkness, or all three. An exact match for her mood at the time. Now she wanted every image of this trip that she could store away in her mind. A seatmate jabbering away at her with inane interruptions was the last thing she needed.

This time—so she told Helen—the trip was to rescue Amy but being a woman who looked carefully and optimistically ahead she did not buy a return ticket. Who knows what opportunity may be presented between now and then.

Chapter 12

Ruff got some water running into the flume a couple of hours after the kid left but it was leaking so much that none made it to the far end. He hunted around for some decently rooted moss to pack into the cracks but soon decided to do like the kid expected of him and let it leak as it soaked the boards overnight. Instead of going directly home he walked along the route the last remaining bit of ditch would follow. In his mind he could see the finished product flowing bank full with clean cool water but not nearly so quickly as the kid insinuated.

So it happened that he was near the road when a car tore by sending a cloud of dust rolling out over him so thickly that he stopped a moment to let it clear. He had been so immersed in his dream of a fast and full flowing stream that he hadn't paid any attention to the car until, as the dust was clearing, he saw it backing up the road toward him. At the point where the road was closest to Ruff the car stopped and the driver climbed out and walked over to him.

"Pardon me, sir, but could you help me out with some directions?"

"Why certainly, if I can."

"I take it that was Spreading Pine that I just passed through. I was expecting it to be a town but it seems to be no more than a sawmill camp. Is that right?"

"Right you are, that was the Spreading Pine alright. Is that what you were looking for?"

"Not exactly though now I understand why everyone local has been adding 'the' in front of it. Actually it's just a route mark on my map. There were several roads leading out from it but this one seemed to go in the right direction to be the road to Dorr. Am I still right?"

"Right as the rain we haven't had all spring." Ruff certainly admired the look of this extremely polite young man. Despite the heat he wore a light coloured suit complete with jacket and a very expensive sort of a high peaked driving cap. Ruff knew it was expensive because he had seen a similar one in town— priced out of his reach—and figured this one was even finer. "If you are heading to Dorr then it's straight ahead and to your right at the first junction you come to. I think there's a sign at the turnoff from that road down to Dorr."

"Well now, that's welcome news. I thank you, Sir, for your kind help." The sporty looking stranger got back into his car and accelerated quickly away as Ruff watched in surprise and envy.

Despite all the wild tales he had heard of the rum runners and their McLaughlin cars he couldn't actually have distinguished one from just about any other make. He knew what his own Studebaker looked like but all others seemed pretty much the same to him. Consequently he just ambled slowly on homeward checking the long finished portion of his ditch—flipping out a fallen limb here and a tumbled stone there or shovelling out a small dirt slide somewhere else. His only thought about the polite and well dressed young man was no more than a murmur in the far back recesses wishing Amy could find such a fine fellow.

He was about halfway home when the shooting started.

Reece had no clue that the unkempt, sweat stained man he talked to was Amy's father though to be truthful, he never looked down on a hard working man. He had done a fair bit of the physical end himself in his younger days when his father ruled with an iron fist and took no backtalk.

He soon slowed, watching for the next road to the left and reminded himself that it might be no more than two tire tracks but should finally take him to Amy.

Amy and Eddy did go for a walk though it took the offer of little Buck for the girl to ride while Eddy walked to get her to go. And she warned she would not go far. It had seemed an innocent thing to entertain Eddy in the kitchen or to brush against him with her shirt tails tied up around her midriff while her father was present to be impressed but was coming to be a different kettle of fish altogether as he grew more sure of himself. She wanted him around in case Reece needed smartening up when he came but she did not want to fall in love with Eddy and she sensed it would be altogether too easy. Eddy represented about the same opportunities into the future for her that her father had for her mother and she wanted none of those hardships and heartaches.

So today she made sure there was little opportunity for conversation by running Buck off this way or that leaving Eddy to walk and talk mostly to himself. But they were walking side by side with Buck following at her heels as they returned just in time for her to see the big black car as it came quietly into the yard on the far side of the house.

Eddy saw nothing but the girl at his side.

Amy knew instantly it was the long awaited Reece for she would recognise that car anywhere. She turned to Eddy with a brilliant smile and began telling him what a marvellous time she had had with him that afternoon. Eddy's heart soared for he had been feeling her remoteness.

When Reece came to his turnoff and swung away from the main road he was surprised to feel his heart beating faster. He even leaned forward as he drove, eager to catch sight of the girl who waited all alone with time passing slowly as she worried and wondered if he ever would come. He actually felt a twinge of guilt for not coming sooner.

It wasn't far, the house came into view at the first corner and he remembered Amy's description. She hadn't been kind to it but even so it was less impressive than he had expected. About to step onto the porch he paused on hearing voices around the far side away from the road he had driven in on. One of those voices he recognised but more to the point—the other one he did not! Three long strides took him to where he saw Amy and a cowboy type approaching from the woods, Amy leading what had to be the other's horse. She was talking animatedly to the cowboy who had eyes for nothing but her.

Reece blew up!

He shouted at the top of his voice, "Amy! What in blazes are you up to? Get yourself over here. Right now! And give the line from that flea bitten crow bait back to that poor, anaemic excuse of a cowboy." His anger was white hot!

She was thrilled! This explosive reaction was even better than she had hoped for. Never before had she dreamed that he had such a temper or could be so obviously jealous.

No question—she had him!

But while she more or less obeyed his command she walked right past him touching his sleeve lightly as she went by. "Calm down, Reece, there's nothing to be angry about. Come into the house and tell me about your trip."

"Angry? If you think I am angry now you just watch awhile!"

At the door she turned but by then he was striding purposefully toward Eddy who had not gotten Buck's reins when she dropped them. The little buckskin, not liking the look of the stranger at all trotted off, head to one side, dragging the reins for a hundred feet before turning to look back. Then he went another fifty feet for good measure before feeling it safe to stand and watch proceedings.

Reece stopped for just a moment, hands on hips, sizing up his prey then made a grab for a stunned and goggle eyed Eddy who had no idea what was wrong but had enough sense to duck away out of arm's reach. He had to keep on backing away as Reece came after him mouthing threats of dismemberment and death without burial to the now thoroughly terrified boy.

With a small worry for Ed's survival now making a slight dent in this otherwise very satisfactory development, Amy ran after them and put herself between them. "For heavens sake, Reece, control yourself. He's just an old friend and nothing more—we went to school together." After this lie she turned to face Eddy, caught her breath and almost laughed at his slack jawed look of dumb fear, "and, Ed, this is Reece, a "—she groped for a word—" a friend from the Coast."

"A "friend" am I! A "friend" is he?" Reece picked Amy up from behind by grasping her arms just below the shoulders, turned with her held six inches off the ground, pointed her toward the house and gave her a shove that nearly sent her sprawling. "Get," he roared at her back, "I'll deal with you later."

She 'got'! Back to the house where she watched from the door while rubbing the hurt from her arms.

Reece swung back and lunged at Eddy who leapt away and ran a half circle toward Buck who was also running a half circle of his own. The horse beat Eddy to the road leading out and whinnied as though saying, "come on Ed, let's get out of here. Home is this way."

With his feet on the road and therefore a clear line of retreat to his horse, added to the comforting knowledge that he could outrun this madman, Eddy stopped.

"I don't understand."

"All you need to understand, simpleton, is that when I get my hands on you I am going to beat you to a pulp that your own mother will disown."

"But, why?" 'Maybe,' he thought, 'if I fight him and he beats me to that pulp then he will be satisfied and won't feel he has to 'deal' with Amy later.'

Eddy had never been in a fight in his life so had no idea how to defend himself never mind how to inflict any damage on the other. At least the white hot, madman anger seemed to be gone now, changed to a cold calculation that might allow Eddy to live beyond the next few minutes however badly beaten. Working to compose his mind for the ordeal, he resolved to go down try-ing—for Amy's sake.

But his new found and still elusive composure deserted him completely and fear took over again as he saw the man Amy called Reece fitting a shiny metal form over the knuckles of his right fist.

'Holy sweet Hannah, this guy means business!'

Eddy backed away again staying just out of reach.

Amy came off the porch toward them. "Cut it out you two," she commanded loudly but neither of them heard her.

"Stand still you twerp or I'll make sure it's all the worse for you when I do catch up to you."

"No. I ain't gonna. I don't want a fight with you. There ain't no point"

"I don't care if you want to or not. I'm going to teach you a lesson you won't forget for the rest of your short and miserable life."

"I reckon you already done that—I just don't understand what that there lesson might be about. Maybe you should tell me about it in words an' then we don't have to work up such a sweat over it."

Amy pulled on Reece's sleeve but got less response than if she had pulled on the limb a big old pine tree.

"I'll teach you a lesson in grammar too while I'm at it. You just keep backing off till those baggy pants trip you up and then we'll get this over with."

After lunging a few more times, jerking Amy along with him without even feeling her grip but still failing to get a hold of the elusive kid, Reece reached within his jacket under his left arm and brought out the wickedest looking snub nose revolver Ed could ever imagine. Of course it was also the first one he had ever seen and here he was looking into the barrel of it while a crazy man held the other end.

Amy gasped and ran for the house. 'I need a club,' she told herself. 'I'll have to hit him over the head to get his attention.' At the moment her sympathy was with Ed who she knew to be no more than the unfortunate victim of her own scheming and could never defend himself against a man like Reece.

"If I can't catch you one way I'll get you another. Now! Stand still!"

Eddy stood still.

In fact he was so petrified with fear that his legs wouldn't have moved for him right then no matter how much he willed them to.

"That's better. Now I think for a warm up I'll see how fast you can dance and if I shoot a few toes off—too bad. Then I am going to shoot out one of your knee caps and once you are down on your back I'll prop up your feet and jump on the other knee. Then we'll see if you can still walk with my girl!"

'Oh God! Amy? Why is this happening?' But of course, he didn't call it out loud and the God he appealed to offered no more help than Ed had ever offered to Him.

Sweat ran down Eddy's face in torrents and his shirt was already soaked. He wondered if he should turn and run hoping to be missed but a second thought warned him this crazy guy probably knows how to shoot.

So he simply turned his back to the man and walked away. He would run without looking back if he heard footsteps coming from behind.

Still a long way to the west, Libby forced her eyes open. All that expensive scenery, to be paid for with extra work, flashing by outside and pure exhaustion was catching up to her.

Chapter 13

Time stood still. It took eons for Ed to drag each foot forward and place it ahead of the other. Half expecting a bullet in the back or—heaven forbid—he wished he hadn't thought of it—a bullet in the back of a knee—he plugged on one foot forward and then the other.

Ten steps and no sound from behind.

Inside the house Amy looked around wildly for something suitable—took up a stick of firewood but dropped it as being too short and too heavy then she spotted the broom.

Fifteen steps.

Twenty steps that Ed was sure must be marked with pools of sweat. Nothing yet!

Reece laughed loud and raucous. "Hey, Skinny, your bravery is showing." More loud and derisive laughter. "Maybe I'll just plug some holes through that spavined hay burner of yours so you have to walk home."

With broom in hand Amy rushed back out just in time to witness Reece firing four fast shots.

Buck jumped aside, snorted and ran off a little farther as one shot kicked gravel over him. All four bullets fell short and erratic the range being too great for the small gun.

Eddy broke into a run too—reached his horse—looked him over quickly for wounds—pulled loose his saddle gun and motioning for Buck to stand still, walked away to one side.

"HEY YOU!"

The older man was already turned away and going toward Amy who had stopped with broom half raised and gripped tight in both hands. He heard the danger in that call and spun back to face Eddy.

"Mister Reece!" Eddy's voice was high and cracking with the fear that rode fast within him yet and the anger that was now boiling over top of it.

"I might not be as big and tough as you are."

"I might not talk too good by your standards."

"I might not know much about good clothes or how to groom my horse to suit you. But by all—I know a bit about short barrelled guns so let's see now who is going to dance the fastest."

And he shot the hat off Reece's head.

It floated away, spinning to the dirt. Reece dived to hide behind his car but it was not a good choice of shelter.

The next shot burst the chrome do-dad perched on the radiator cowl to a hundred ragged bits of pot metal.

The third shot shattered the glass of the driver's side headlight leaving an oblong exit hole in the rounded back of the headlamp assembly.

The fourth was aimed at the other headlamp but cold sanity was lurking yet in Eddy's mind—he wanted both the car and it's driver capable of leaving. If he shot the passenger side headlight with the car parked at the angle it was the bullet would go on into the engine compartment and might do crippling damage.

He shifted to the fancy rear view mirror attached to the passenger side door post—there was one on the driver's side too—it disappeared as the bullet passed on into the car through the open passenger side window and plowed a hole out the curved, opposite rear corner spraying Reece with small particles of something.

118

One shot more and he would have to reload. Eddy held fire while a corner of his mind counted the spare bullets in his belt loops—no shortage.

Amy, flumoxed by the sudden turn of events, slowly lowered the broom but otherwise stood frozen.

Reece hadn't counted the shots but hoped the pause meant 'out of ammunition'. He started out from behind the car but made the mistake of coming gun hand first with the revolver held at the ready. His hand with the gun in it was barely a foot beyond the dubious shelter of the car when his revolver blew to pieces. The revolving cylinder that held the cartridges was ripped from the frame by Ed's bullet and spun wildly across the yard kicking up a trail of dust. The barrel and the frame went flying too but not as far. Reece screamed in agony and rolled over and over on the ground his good left hand grasping the wrist of the injured one.

Amy, stabbed to the heart with a sudden unexpected and un-explainable fear by that cry, dropped the broom, ran to Reece and knelt on the ground between him and Ed. Now that she had won him she would shelter him from more bullets with her own body if she had to. She grabbed his good hand where it clutched his right wrist and held him still so she could see the damage. At one point she looked toward Eddy to find him calmly reloading his rifle and her allegiance completed its latest shift of sides—her man was down.

"Coward," she screamed, "I hate you!"

She struggled with the injured man trying to keep him from banging his hand against the ground in his agony. Eventually she got him sitting up and held on and rocked back and forth with him.

She screamed at Ed again as he picked the ejected brass cas-ings from the ground and shoved them into empty loops in his belt. "Come back here you coward and fight like a man."

"No, Amy, I can't fight him now, he has shot off my hand! I may bleed to death."

Startled, Amy looked Reece in the face to discover he had his eyes shut tight.

"No, Reece, it's okay. It's all there—open your eyes."

He did—took one brief look and fell over sideways against her in a dead faint. She held him tight and looked Eddy's way. He was leaving—walking toward his horse.

"Eddy, come back. Please—I need help."

She did not call it out loudly but Eddy heard though he walked on to Buck and sheathed the hammerless Savage—the faulty gun that could never be expected to shoot accurately. Then, reluctantly, he went to Amy.

Reece was awake by the time Ed got there and rocking back and forth again but he was quiet now. Ed, faced with what he had done was appalled. The slightest miss and he would have killed this man—blown his head wide open. Had that happened Amy would now be covered with blood and brains. He trembled uncontrollably and it was only partly from righteous anger released.

"Aw. Amy—Reece. I'm sorry. I shouldn't of done that." He thought again of those four quick shots aimed at Buck. "But you made me mad."

In Eddy's mind that unintentional linking of their names was as symbolic and as final as a wedding ceremony. The heart that a few short minutes ago, had soared—now crashed. Had Amy looked into his eyes right then she would have seen it breaking.

"Help me get him into the car."

"Why not to the house and put that hand in a bucket of cold water?"

"No! He's got to have a doctor. A real doctor and not that half baked quack they have at the sawmill." The 'half baked quack at the sawmill' would be Errol the timekeeper who, as first aid man for the operation, made initial repairs to injured workers before shipping them off to hospital.

"Just help me up."

120

Between the two of them they got Reece on his feet though his balance was not good and he would have fallen sideways had Ed not held him up.

"Don't handle a little pain too good do you."

"A little pain! Man, if only you knew! My arm seems to end at the elbow then there's nothing but fire beyond that. I've read stories of old time gunslingers shooting a gun out of some desperado's hand and then they have a fist fight like there was no injury. Believe me—this is not a bit like that!"

Pushing away from Ed but with Amy still holding on to him Reece went to the driver's door of the McLaughlin. There he stopped and looked so confused that it seemed he might break down and cry.

"I can't drive!"

Amy, confounded, looked at Ed. Ed blinked and looked away.

"It's not just the hand—I can't see straight—everything is spinning on me. I think I'm going to be sick." He sat heavily on the running board with a lean to the right as though his sense of balance had deserted him again. With Amy holding his head he donated his Elko lunch to the parched soil of Ruff's Prairie. Eddy, skeptical till now, was finally convinced that Reece was not pretending his helplessness. In the same instant he lost all fear of this man who had been so easily brought down to size with not even a visible bleeding wound. The monster now was not only manageable but actually in need of help and help was something Eddy was always ready to give. Besides, if Amy is in love with this man then there must be some good hidden within him. Eddy would never think of the dollar signs.

"Let's get him around to the other side, Amy, and I will drive him to a doctor."

"You? But—."

"Yes. Somebody has to. You can't drive and Ruff ain't here," 'though after all that shooting he soon will be if he has a brain in his head,' "so I got to."

"Can he drive?"

"Yes, Reece, he is a good driver—your car will like him." She stopped talking abruptly and hoped he would not ask her to explain that or how she knew for such a certainty about Ed's driving. The world was spinning again for Reece so she got away with it.

"I got to turn Buck loose so he can go home. I'll be back in a couple of minutes."

"But, he is loose."

"No, Amy, he ain't. He's still got the bridle on. I'll take it off and tie it to the saddle and then he can go."

By the time Eddy returned Reece was seated on the passenger's side leaning against Amy who stood as close as she could get to him at the open door. As Ed slipped behind the steering wheel Amy pushed Reece upright, closed the door and opened the back door to climb in.

"No, you stay here. Your father needs to find you home."

"I'll leave a note—it will only take a minute."

"We don't need you along—he can sleep or whatever he wants."

"He's right, Amy. I'll be fine in a while. I don't know how long we will be but I'll be back as soon as I can."

Reluctantly she closed the door and stood back to watch them leaving. "So, Reece, I have found a crack in your hard shell and I love it." She backed up her thoughts to examine that word 'love'—such a sneaky emotional thing—never to be trusted but for the moment she would leave it alone. She did not yet understand that something momentous had happened to her in the yard today far beyond the witnessing of a gun fight—Eddy would approve of the missing dollar signs.

Without lifting his nose from the grass he was nibbling at around a clump of sage brush, little Buck watched too. When the car was out of sight he snorted, bucked and bolted away as if cracked by a whip. At full gallop, stirrups tied together over the saddle, he set a true course for home.

If Amy noticed that Ed swung the McLaughlin south instead of north then she must have thought he was going the longer route for Reece's sake—a smoother road.

The four fast shots got Ruff's attention but did not alarm him, working outdoors all day as he did, he often heard shots. Shooting in the area was almost an everyday occurrence—it might be no more than some kid target practising. Somebody was always potting gophers or a coyote or even poaching a deer for the table. Year round shooting of deer was so common that few thought of it as poaching at all. It was just a thing that half the families around did as a matter of every day life. Nearly everyone, especially those who had no family member with a paying job, ate the King's beef—or as some called it—gunny sack beef.

Ruff had a good working knowledge of guns in their many forms and he recognised these shots as coming from a small handgun but even that was not so unusual for there were lots of them around legal or not and often someone practising their marksmanship. The next salvo sounded to be from about the same direction but because right then he was within a dense thicket and a curve of the hillside, the sound was broken up and he took it to be farther away than it really was. Those four evenly spaced rifle shots would be someone shooting at running game—the fifth shot later would be the finishing off. Someone has their deer or their coyote.

For some obscure reason the shooting reminded Ruff of the letter inside his shirt so he sat down, felt around his waist and brought it out sweat stained and grimy. But it was the envelope with the ten dollar bills that he had in his hand. He stared at it—amazed that he could have so completely forgotten about it and the reason that he had it. A clear sign, he feared, that his mind was no longer keeping proper connection between events. He shoved it back inside his shirt and fished for the other envelope.

A telegram—sent by the Elko Station Agent—a short one. Worse yet—from Libby! It read -

HE GOT AWAY STOP AM COMING STOP TRAIN 30TH STOP

The thirtieth! Tomorrow!
Libby here too? "Just what I need!"
And no gas for the car!
Then he started worrying—'what if that was Libby's 'gangster' who was asking directions a little while ago? It was a black car. Couldn't possibly be—he was much too pleasant and polite. Even to a dirty old—well, not all that old—ditch digger he was respectful. Couldn't be.'
All the same Ruff became suddenly in a hurry to get home.
At home the yard was quiet and empty—no extra car or people to be seen. No horse either—that was good. But it was go-dawful quiet until he heard the oven door in the kitchen whump down. Stepping inside he found it so stifling hot from the cook stove despite the open door and windows that he nearly backed out to the yard again.
"We'll have to eat outside in the shade tonight, Father. I've warmed up the last of the beef roast that we have been eating cold and made one of your favourites to go with it. How does Yorkshire pudding and gravy sound?"
On this hot evening—with the added heat of Libby arriving on the scene altogether too soon—Ruff would rather have it cold. But—Yorkshire pudding! And gravy!
"Sounds good to me, Amy."
He thought, 'a few things are right in this old world yet. Maybe she will be in a good enough mood that I can tell her that her mother is coming and why.'
She thought, 'it's worth it if it puts him in a good enough mood so I can prepare him for tomorrow when Reece should be back. And when I will be leaving.'

Chapter 14

Reece came upright as Eddy slowed to turn off on a rutted side road. "What now? Where does this go?"

"To the best doctor in the country. That's what you want isn't it?"

"On a road like this? I don't believe you."

"I don't tell lies."

"If you say so." Reece nodded as though accepting that simple statement as being the truth even though in his experience everyone told lies. The trick was to catch them at it and he was good at doing so. Right now he was just too weak, tired, and sick to worry much about it.

That unexpected acceptance of such a broad statement so unnerved Eddy that he had to wiggle around with it a little. "Aw. I might bend the truth a wee mite now and then or find a way to tell less than the whole of it. I might pull your leg a bit but I don't out and out lie. There really is a good doctor lives out this road—she just don't have no letters behind her name is all."

They were passing a house and barn with corrals and smaller out buildings—a woman in the yard stared at the car as it passed. It was not one she recognised so she didn't wave until Ed waved at her. So then she did wave but with caution since he was on the

125

far side from her and she, not used to seeing him in a car, was unsure.

Reece, watching it all, mentally shook his head. 'What a poor and destitute existence,' he thought. 'This must be about the way Amy grew up. It might be why she stands out so in a crowd. It has shaped her but she is too strong to accept such a life and has taken steps beyond it though she is too honest to deny it's where she comes from. 'Honest she might be but she lied to me today when she said that she and Ed went to school together. She hoped to keep me from tearing him apart.'

An honest lie? No such thing exists. A well intentioned lie perhaps and her actions through the rest of the incident certainly left no doubt of her loyalty. Just a day ago he might have considered her caught in trespass but now he felt drawn closer. There had been no other weapon or resource available to her at that moment—it's what he might have tried himself if put in her place.

"Who lives here?"

"That's Chuck and Myrtle's place—our closest neighbours except for my sister and her husband. That was Myrtle that waved."

Reece scowled then almost smiled. "It's good of you to mention that—I might have thought it was Chuck."

"You must be feeling better."

"It doesn't hurt any less but yes, I think I could get out and walk a straight line now if I had to." And so he could lie too when he felt it was necessary. He could hold his head upright now and his vision was steadying but an unassisted walk may not be so easy as he had implied though he was not going to admit such a handicap to Eddy.

"That's good, 'cause I sure wasn't planning to pack you to the house."

Reece hoped fervently that by the time they got to the house, wherever it is, he would indeed be able to walk something resembling a straight line. For perhaps the very first time in his life he was genuinely frightened and becoming more so as each

126

turn of this atrocious road took them deeper into the woods and farther away from what he saw as the safety of the open road and other people. It was a fear that grew in large part from the helpless feeling of his own body as well as whatever unknowns might lay ahead on this poor road. Illogically, he also feared the scrawny kid who, as they both well knew, was now in the driver's seat in every meaning of the words. 'I could thrash him with one hand tied behind my back if I was healthy but he tricked me. I should have known he might have a gun on his saddle but it's a thing outside my experience.' Experience within his father's crowd had taught him that the impression of mental toughness backed by physical strength added up to safety. But that looked to be a hard sell to pull off right now. Only recently had he started learning there were other ways—that sometimes a smile and a pleasant word got you farther. Politeness and good manners had become such a successful tool for him that now both came quite naturally unless his temper overruled. An invitation to casual conversation could open doors—keep Eddy talking and he will have less time to think up mischief.

"This woman doctor you are taking me to—why does she—'have no letters after her name'?"

"Aw. I reckon 'cause she never asked for any—never went and took any exams or whatever. For that matter I reckon she never took any training but don't let no little detail like that bother you cause she ain't lost no patients yet either. Course I reckon someday there will be a first one."

"And you are hoping that first one will be me."

"Well—."

The right side wheels banged through a couple of deep potholes just then but Reece had seen them coming in time to lift his sore arm up in front of him to ride out the jolting in mid air. He was almost certain Ed had steered to hit the holes rather than to miss them.

"No. I reckon not. Wouldn't want word to get around that she finally had to bury one."

"I'm certainly glad to hear that!"

"Hey. Don't worry. She's stitched up some pretty fair gashes and set and splinted most of the bones that been busted around close by. She has even sewed over some stumps where fingers or toes got chopped. An arm once too that got shoved into a hay baler when it shouldn't of—good enough to get on to the hospital without bleeding to death at any rate. Or maybe it was a thrash machine, I was pretty small at the time and don't remember it too clear but this'll be a piece of cake for her."

"Nobody I would know, of course, but I could use a name."

"Well. To me she's Ma—or Reb if she ain't standing too close. To you I reckon she will have to be Mrs. Cameron. If you get along real good with her you might try Reb too."

"Your Mother?"

"The same and only one I know of."

"I don't like this, Ed! What could she know about a thing like this?"

"Prob'ly never seen the likes before in her life of a grown man having such a conniption fit over a hand no more than gone to sleep. You always faint when you get a hand slapped or was you just looking for sympathy since there was a nice handy lap to lay your head on?"

"Watch it, sonny, I've still got one good hand." Bluff had always been a part of his game.

"And I got a hold of the steering wheel of this here fancy car and there's lots of trees handy to smack it into while I grab that sore paw to see if it really hurts."

"Just pay attention to your driving and I'll try to keep my 'paws' off of you."

Eddy turned onto an even more doubtful track that switchbacked and climbed back along the hillside above the road they had just negotiated. Soon even that deteriorated at a junction where the most used route continued the same uphill grade. Here Ed swerved left to a way through the trees on which the most significant improvement was little more than a mark scratched along the high side for the uphill tires to follow.

"Ever had a car in here before?" Reece was worried now for his car as well as for himself and held his injured hand out in mid air again to where it was least likely to make contact with any solid object as Eddy eased them along over rocks and around stumps."

"Sure. Once. Just the other day to be exact."

"I suppose it's still in here and can't get out."

"Sit easy, Reece, we'll get your car back out and old Reb will either fix your hand or send us along to where they know how to cut it open and tinker with the inner works if that's what is needed."

"Thanks, I feel better already." They came to a clearing where the dominating structure, space wise, seemed to be the horse corrals. "This is where you live?"

"This is her."

"Where is the house?"

"Right in front of you."

"That log—shack?"

"Yup. Guess you weren't expecting anything so grand."

"Uh, no. One room?"

"It's sort of halfway divided to two inside. Plenty big enough for Reb. I sleep in the penthouse suite of that there harness shed little Buck is trying to break into to see if he can kill himself with a feed of oats. Funny thing about horses—real smart—until it comes to a bit of grain and then no self control at all."

"Go ahead on in the house and see if Reb is home while I take care of Buck before he figures out how to untwist that there haywire."

"I'll wait for you."

"Shoot yourself."

Ed stripped saddle and blanket from Buck but left it on the ground in front of the closed and wired shed door. Buck pushed him all the way to the corral gate, rushed inside when it was opened, raced to the water trough where he splashed his nose just once in passing as he buck jumped his way to the hay manger where Ed was filling it for him. The little horse sniffed loudly in the grain box at one end of the manger, rolled his eyes and made as if he would bite Ed through the rails when no grain was offered. Accepting second prize he shoved his nose into the hay, swirling it around violently working the fines down to the bottom where, eye deep in good green hay, he licked at the best stuff first. While Ed had the shed door open to put away the saddle Buck lifted his head just enough so he could watch every move through a space between the rails. He lost interest and plunged back into his timothy when the shed door was swung shut.

While Ed cared for his horse Reece made his way to the house where he could lean against a wall to hide his untrustworthy balance.

"Come on inside but I don't think she's home or Buck would have been cared for."

"Where would she be?"

"Oh. Not far I reckon. Prob'ly up at my sister's place helping out at something or other."

In such a small house no searching or calling was needed to confirm that, indeed, Reb was not at home.

"Dog-gone! And only an hour to eating time. This could get plumb stressful. I'll have to go hunting for her—just set yourself easy there at the table—won't be long."

Ed only made about two steps outside the open door—stopped and backed in again. "She's coming."

Reece had set himself carefully on a laced hide chair at the table and found it more comfortable than he had expected but wondered about the table. Should he think of it as 'kitchen' table? Or dinning room table? This room served both purposes and living room as well yet despite it's small size, there was very little clutter in it. The woman coming—what would she be like? He looked at Ed lifting lids from canisters along the back of a wide shelf. Looking for what? Hidden cookies? A little boy almost grown to a man—or a grown man masquerading as a little boy in those too big for him pants. Cheeky as all getout yet strangely respectful at times. Don't push him for he is made of spring steel hidden in soft cloth and tricky to boot—a discovery Reece had made too late. 'That first shot—I thought he aimed to kill me but missed—now I know that every bullet went exactly where he wanted it to. He was just doing to me his version of what I did to him. If our roles had been reversed I'm not sure I could have been so level headed and generous as to keep that bullet high when inches lower might be easily justified as self defence. But the risk the fool ran! With my life!'

Reece knew he had never come closer to death and he guessed his mind was as much in shock by that as his body was in shock from his injury. He prided himself on being quick to read the character of people at first meeting but had to admit he had tripped up with Ed. Didn't have him figured out yet. He found that both intriguing and frightening. Was the kid still thinking revenge when the time and place might be more right? 'Perhaps I am to go missing and Amy will be told that I have gone without her. Or is all this rough pleasantry and offhand helpfulness a way of saying he is sorry?

The woman was close enough now that he could hear a whisper of her footsteps—her son looked to be part Indian—would the mother be a full blood? Just what kind of a doctor anyway? Would she speak English? Reece squirmed forward to the edge of the chair as if ready to run for it though he would never admit to such a thing—couldn't run now anyway. The steps slowed as she neared the open door that had been closed when she left. She would know from the car parked outside that a stranger was in her house waiting but she should also have seen Buck in the corral.

Ed's mother, when she entered her house, completely shattered all Reece's wild and fearful expectations. Except for the moccasins on her feet and heavy, men's style work socks showing above them she was dressed almost exactly as his own mother dressed to work in her garden or flower beds. About the same as all the women in the block dressed for their yard work. He felt instantly at ease with her before she said one word and as he settled back in the chair he knew that she was relieved by the look of him too though not as fully comfortable about it as he. Not every day does a McLaughlin Buick Six settle to rest in her yard.

"Bout time you got home, Reb. Here it is almost time to eat and you been out traipsing about the countryside as if you had all day for playing among the flowers."

"If you are so eager for supper perhaps you should get your fingers out of the cookie jar and quit spoiling your appetite. Or at least offer some to your guest too." Her voice was so soft and musical that one had to listen closely to get all that she said.

"Oh. Yeah. Forgot about him. This here is Reece. He's a friend over at Ruff's and he's had a bit of a axledent. Needs you to look at his hand."

Reb had already seen the hand held awkwardly to keep it neither hanging downward for blood pressure to build in nor where it might bump something. She saw no visible wounds but the hand was swollen and discoloured—the wrist puffy.

"Yes, we had better attend to that right away. Would you care to place it on the table between us," she said as she settled herself in a chair across from him.

Reece studied this 'doctor without letters' while she studied his hand without reaching out to touch it. Entirely different than he had been imagining since learning he was being taken to Ed's mother. Much too young to fit the role—still in her thirties he would bet and showing no more hint of mixed blood than her son. Tall for a woman and almost as thin as Eddy but—such a lovely face—with kindness in every glance.

"Would you put your other hand out alongside it please so I can compare."

She had still not touched his hand.

"Can you straighten the fingers out?"

132

To anyone else he would have said 'no'—indignantly. For her he tried and nearly succeeded.

"That's enough. Let it lie in the position you find most comfortable." He let the fingers slowly back to the cupped position that hurt the least. At last she reached out but to the good left hand instead of the injured one and with one finger traced out the bone structure.

"You have very sensitive hands."

His own doctor back home had put it differently—'*you have glass hands my boy.-*'

"Such long and delicate fingers."

'—*you had better quit hitting people or you will become my best customer.*'

"Not many have such fine and supple wrists."

'*Your wrist is not built to stand what your arm and shoulder can dish out.*'

"Are you a musician?"

'*I'll try to convince your father that you are not cut out to be his enforcer.*'

The old man ranting, '*no kid of mine is allowed to have "glass hands"—strap on a leather wrist brace and get yourself some good heavy brass knuckles.*'

"Not exactly." 'I wonder where my knuckles have gotten to? Probably somewhere in Amy's yard. Hope she doesn't find them.'

"But you would like to be. You have a liking for a certain stringed instrument."

Reece blinked rapidly. "Yes, I did once have that notion."

'*You can get that stupid notion out of your head right now— no kid of mine is going to make a fool of me by taking up music.*' What a pity the old man had only one kid.

"But I developed no skill at it."

'I wasn't allowed to.'

At last she took the injured hand in both of hers and explored it's shape and structure as she had done with the good one. "Open

133

your eyes and look at me so I can tell when I hurt you too much." She spoke with a slow precision that implied English might not be her language of preference.

He opened his eyes and stared at the tip of her nose. Side vision—just before it dissolved in pain—told him Ed was watching. He steeled himself to not lose sight of the very beautiful face in front of him—the face that became even more beautiful as the deep brown eyes filled with compassion. As long as he could see that face everything would be alright—there would be no pain that he could not endure—he would feel nothing—nothing at all—.

"That's fine, you can relax now."

Reece, proud of not passing out, looked to Ed for approval but found him, back turned, getting out dishes and cutlery from a cupboard—hinting that it's time to quit fooling around and get a meal on the table. 'Now why would I look to that skinny dumbbell for approval?' But deep down he knew why—the skinny dumbbell had beaten him at his own game.

"I've had this before or at least something similar, they usually put it in a cast." 'In which it swells more and hurts more—then itches as the cast becomes loose.'

"No bones are broken or if they are then they are not out of alignment so you don't need a cast. There is deep bruising and the wrist might be sprained somewhat. By the time this is over with you might be wishing it was just a few simple fractures. They might heal faster than this will."

"It seldom heals quickly," he agreed.

"Edward, I will tend to the table and the meal. I want you to go to the woodpile and split a thin shake for me, like so," she indicated a quarter inch between thumb and forefinger, "so long and so wide—gestures with both hands. Make it smooth—no slivers—shaped so it will fit your friend's hand like this," she demonstrated with her own cupped hand and a cribbage board she reached for to simulate the splint. "Only it must be much thinner and lighter. You should go with him so he can fit it to your hand and wrist as he makes it."

"Hey I ain't no sculptor."

"'I am not a sculptor', if you please," she chided. You know better. You know what I want too."

"Okay, Reb, I got the message. Guess this means food will be ready when we get back?"

She smiled indulgently at her son and then at Reece too to let him know he was included, "it does."

Outside, Ed split, shaved, trimmed and shortened a piece of dry larch to the shape his mother had called for. Next, while Reece sat on a block of wood and held his breath at every touch, he fitted it roughly to the shape of the injured hand with a little extra carving.

"That was quick."

"Hey. Things happen fast when supper is waiting."

"This isn't going to work, you know"

"If Reb says it will work—it will work."

"Now don't get snotty about it. I'm just thinking a real cast might be best since it would be more form fitting and"—he had the grace to pause and look doubtful—"comfortable."

"Tomorrow you can go wherever you like and have whatever you want done to it. Might be you think if you throw enough dollars at it it will feel better but personally I think different. In fact, I'd still say a bucket of cold water is what it needs. Reb is just being polite in not saying so."

"Oh. You're worried that I won't pay her are you? On the other hand it's your fault that this has happened so maybe you should do the paying."

"Keep wobbling your tongue like that while I got a knife in my hand and you'll be back in there for more repairs."

They were both quiet while Ed worked at the last of the shaping.

"Mister Reece?"

"What?"

"Might be that I am kind of dumb and stupid in your eyes and I reckon you might be more than half right about that but I can give you one good hint if you want it."

"I'm listening."

"If Reb says you owe her something then you can consider paying up but whatever you think—DO NOT ASK."

"If she doesn't give me a bill and I don't ask how do I know what to pay?"

"Most people wouldn't see no problem with that. Some might drop by later with a deer hide or two for her and maybe a hind quarter to boot. Some might just think well of her once in a while and sometimes I think that's the pay she likes best."

"What would she do with a deer hide?"

"Aw. Reece. You are plumb dumb in your own fancy way. She'd tan it and make things for us to wear—like moccasins for example"

"I don't see you wearing moccasins."

"Well. No. This dumb Indian thinks he's a cowboy and so has to dress the part accordingly. There you go, all done. A personalised fit if I do have to say it myself. Might be, while you think nice things about Reb, you could also think about pumping one less bullet into me."

"Ed?"

"Um."

"I've got an idea."

"I hope it's better than any you've had so far today."

"Have you got any way to drill a small hole in the middle of this, right under where the palm of my hand will be?"

"Reckon I might. I could stab and carve a hole with my knife but Percy has a drill in his shed. We could go up there—after we eat. Why the hole? To let the blood drain out after Reb cinches it up tight on you?"

"Of course not! I was just thinking—"

"Dangerous. When you ain't equipped for it."

"—that if I removed the glass ball on the gear shift and had a hole in this to fit over the threaded iron rod part I could drive halfway normal even with this. I'm always steering with one hand anyway."

"Good thought! The best you ever had that I know about. That there will free me of you so I can get on with my own business which you have already put into serious jeopardy by using up my time this afternoon. Might be if Reb don't present you with a bill—I should."

Reece opened his mouth, closed it, then tightened up his expression before a smile could form. Things were definitely looking up—between Eddy's strange humour and his mother's helpful concern he was starting to feel more like a guest than the prisoner he had thought he was.

"Let's see how the cook is doing before we head up the hill."

"Of course."

Chapter 15

It wasn't much of a shop. More a storage place for hand tools but there was a forge, an anvil and an old hand crank post drill with a good assortment of drill bit sizes though not actually the kind meant for drilling wood. Ed turned the crank with one hand while very slowly advancing the bit with his other hand. He clicked the top wheel cautiously past it's stop dog one notch at a time with the automatic advance pawl thrown back. With his good hand Reece held his brace to keep it from revolving with the bit. Watching the side wheels spin made him a bit dizzy but since eating with Ed and his mother he felt much better—his balance was okay now—he was just very tired, weak and a bit trembly which might be as much from his long hours of driving yesterday. Having met and talked with Eddy's mother he no longer feared for his safety though he knew his position was still one of considerable disadvantage. Incredible as it might seem he and Ed were almost on friendly terms even if there were depths and shallows to it for both of them. Unquestionably Eddy had been scared to death this afternoon and his reactions had been far from heroic until he got to his rifle. He might be touchy about that for a while. Reece felt no pride in his own performance either. He had reverted instantly to the hardcase his father had trained him to be. The 'Enforcer' out to strike abject terror into his victim of the moment and very good at it too until his wonky hands and wrists became apparent. 'Seeing Amy and Eddy together—after imagining her alone and worried—.'

"Got to do this slow—tamarack splits too easy along the grain if you force it. Don't want to have to start from scratch again. Should have made it from pine."

A figure stepping in at the doorway cut off some of the dim light that they worked by—both of them turned.

"Ed, Percy is home tonight and—oh—I thought you were alone."

"Hi there, Het, it's okay, come on back in. This here is Reece, he's a friend from over at Ruff's. A friend of the Ruff's that is—not of mine. Sorry 'bout that Reece—didn't come out quite like I intended. Anyhow this is my sister Hettie."

The girl edged forward about half way into the doorway she had just sidestepped away from and they nodded to each other but she wouldn't lift her eyes from the floor.

"What was you saying about Percy?"

"He's home tonight, we heard you cranking the drill and he says to come up for a coffee. He worked twelve hours today and then walked four miles to get home so he is tired but he wants to visit for a while. I've got two pies and some cake too."

Hey, favourite Sis, you couldn't keep us away, right, Reece?"

Reece nodded but while Eddy visualised coffee, pie and cake—he was looking at the girl.

"Then I will expect you up soon." She shied away out of sight around the door's edge far too aware of Reece's stare.

"She's shy, just like your mother, only more so."

"Well. Reb shy? I sure never noticed."

"Not for you I wouldn't think but for a stranger she certainly is."

"Aw. I reckon they don't get out to see people like I do. I know about everybody from the Elk River down to the Tobacco

River in Montana and a few from beyond—both ways—but Hettie digs her heels in here at home. Reb has her friends and people are often brought to her in times of trouble but she don't go nowhere much neither."

"She says you know better."

"Say now. She tries hard but you don't need to get in on the act too. You're on shaky enough ground around here now."

"You sure didn't learn all that 'ain't' and 'don't nohow' stuff from her."

Aw. Reece. In this modern day it's plumb too easy to be just another pea in the pod. Sometimes a dumb cowboy has to work real hard to be his own self."

"You must have been a handful for your school teacher."

"Aw. I reckon. But I didn't bother her for long. Even old Reb got in more grades than me."

"Where do you have to go to find a school around here?"

"Well. There's always been a little old one room schoolhouse within hiking or riding distance—even way back in the old days when Reb was a kid."

"That would do it."

"And you? Can't allow you to dig without filling."

"What? Oh. Well, the very best my mother could arrange to the very soonest my dad could end it."

"Figures. My old father was like that too. Well. We are done here so let's go help out with that pie problem that has Percy boxed in so bad he is crying out for help."

"You go ahead. That invitation was for you. I'm going down with this thing you made for me and have your mother strap it on whatever way she has in mind and then I will see if I can get my car back out of here."

"And where do you think you are off to at this time of evening?"

"Why—."

"Exactly. No use goin' to Ruff's cause they ain't got a room for you."

"No, I can't go there until tomorrow now."

"You might find a room in Elko if you can thread your way through all those, hell-bent-to-get-drunk-quick-as-they-can loggers that are already pouring in there what with this bein' the start of a weekend."

"Don't they work tomorrow?"

"The mills do but lots of the loggers work extra hours through the week so they can have two days off—like Percy has done. Makes it more worthwhile to come in out of the bush."

"Is Fernie any closer than Cranbrook?"

"It is too. Road ain't much though. Been closed a lot on account of high water in some creeks. Might be hot and dry here but this same fine weather is melting snow like crazy high up. I wouldn't even dream to try it in the dark. Or might be you like the idea of running strange and dangerous roads with one hand and one headlight."

"Not really. I hadn't thought about that headlamp yet—or my mirror or my chrome falcon—but I'm going to."

"Just add 'em to my account. Reckon it's back up one bullet. Think you know the way from here to Elko good enough to find your way in the dark? Or even just back to Ruff's?"

"No! Blast your smart alec hide. I was in a fog most of the way here—I haven't a clue where I am."

"Thought so. You might figure it out in daylight but that being the unpalatable case, I reckon we are stuck with you for the night."

"You have a room I can use?"

"Sure. You just got to share my top floor suite but I won't slit your throat through the night while you sleep."

"Just you try it wise guy."

"Nope. Just promised I wouldn't. But. Seeing as you are stranded here you might as well make the best of it and have some pie and cake along with me and Percy before today serves notice it has become yesterday."

It turned out rather short as visits go. Hettie had the table set for them and loaded with things that should only be eaten in moderation this near bed time but Percy was falling asleep in his chair. He pulled himself a little awake as his wife came from the other room and went to the stove for the coffee pot but he truly looked as though he needed toothpicks to prop his eyelids open. He accepted Reece just as Eddy introduced him—'a friend from over at Ruffs'—and showed no curiosity in the man's presence at all as if he were completely accustomed to Eddy dragging home various and sundry at any time.

"He's got a sore hand but Reb is taking care of it."

Reece was little more than a silent, impatient and barely interested spectator although the interest grew slightly because of the exotic (to him) topics as they discussed the abundance of weather over the last month and the prospects of more and worse over the next month. They also complained about the shortage of groceries in the form of whitetail deer—a circumstance compounded since only the bucks were fair game at this time of year. Obviously he was in the company of two inveterate and unrepentant poachers—poachers who would never dream the word might apply to them. To them, to judge by their indignant appraisal of a recent incident, a poacher was one who killed an animal and then wasted it. Reece, on the other hand, lived mostly indoors where weather was not a factor. He had never lifted a finger in his life to procure groceries of any type. Most particularly not the fleet footed wild variety either for his mother at home or for his places of business.

"Sorry fellas, I was fine till I sat down and relaxed to my supper but now working all week in that heat has caught up to me and has hit like a ton of bricks." He put both hands to the table's edge as though to push himself away but lifted one to cover his cup as Hettie came again to top up their coffee. "No more for me, Het, it would take more than coffee to keep me awake now."

Reece had been watching the girl with open admiration but something about Percy—some subtle shift in body language

142

now caught his attention. The man had turned slightly to Hettie and looked up at her with nothing less than sleepy eyed little boy wonder—a total adoration of this most important person in his world. As she moved to pass on around the end of the table she touched the fingers of her free hand to the hand that Percy still rested on the table edge. Even cold minded, hard edged Reece sensed the oneness of this unlikely pair—young girl and middle aged man. He felt as though he and Eddy had been granted a peek through a window at a very private and intimate interlude. In fact, he felt that he should not be here at all or at the very least should look away for the moment but was unable to do so. The act before him now went into slow motion—Percy sliding his hand along the table edge and Hettie's arm stretching to it's limit—both of them intent on making the contact last as long·as possible. Reece fully expected an electric spark to jump from one to the other when contact was broken but if such a thing happened then he missed it for he had to blink his eyes at that instant.

As Hettie reached to refill his half empty cup Reece did the same as Percy had done and covered it with one hand but Eddy shoved his own cup forward to make it easier for his sister to fill. After replacing the pot on the stove she went to the next room. There she could be heard and occasionally seen getting her children ready for bed by the faint light of a kerosene lamp similar to the one on the kitchen table—full darkness having come in the short time they had been visiting.

"Tired, huh."

"Man, I'll say! Don't leave on my account but I am done in for today. I just may sleep till noon tomorrow."

Percy stood and made his way to the door leading outside and though he zigged once when he should have zagged he made it and the screen door slapped shut behind him.

"Let's go," Reece suggested starting to rise.

"Sit. I ain't done yet."

"I am and it's time we left these people alone."

"Percy will be back in a minute and we should be right here to say a nice pleasant good night to him."

Reece saw some merit in that suggestion and settled down in his chair.

The outside air had little effect on Percy, if anything, he appeared even sleepier as he came in and went directly through to the other room. "Might see you tomorrow, boys."

"Sure thing Percy, don't sleep too late, might get to be a bad habit."

"Good night, Percy." All considered it came out pretty decent Reece thought.

"Now we go."

"Nope. You sit right there while I finish snacking. Have some more yourself."

"How long does this go on?"

"Well." Ed surveyed the table in front of him. "I'd like to say until the table is empty but if you are done—- I ain't too sure I can handle it all alone."

"You're crazy!"

"Glad you finally noticed. Everyone else has."

Ed very carefully slid another slice of pie onto his plate, sipped coffee and smiled his pleasure at the taste of it. Reece had found it too strong for his liking but now he lifted his cup, tested again and even reached for another piece of cake.

Eventually Ed pushed back from the table and his sister came so immediately that Reece knew she had been watching from the shadows at the farthest end of the other room and was probably wishing for their departure.

"More coffee Ed?" She did not say Reece's name—perhaps she had forgotten it—but the wave of the coffee pot and her smile included him in the offer.

"Nope. Should sleep warm and secure now with knowing there's a fair chance we won't starve to death before breakfast."

"I've had more than enough too, Mrs.—" and there he floundered until she helped him out, "Stuart," and he started again,

144

"—Mrs. Stuart. I have to say, that was the best cake I've had in ages." He smiled as gallantly for her as for any other pretty girl but did not mention the coffee.

"Thank you, I'm glad you liked it."

They walked in a stony silence more than half way back to Reb's house.

"You could have told me their name in advance."

"You never asked."

Reb was waiting for them with her lamp lit and placed at the centre of the table where she examined the brace Ed had made. She looked at but did not question the drilled hole in the palm end of it. Off to the side where the light was poor a mostly black cat, little more visible than a ghost, suddenly attacked a pair of high topped boots that must be Ed's. It seized a lace in it's mouth and backed away shaking it from side to side until the boot, with the lace drawn tight, fell over toward the cat. It vanished into the darkness where it's eyes flashed green fire as it guarded it's back trail.

"I have this little bag of filler," she did not explain what it was, "to fit in the palm of your hand while the fingers go mostly over the end. This should keep your hand as comfortable as possible for now and yet allow you to flex the fingers for exercise which you should do quite often."

The bag of filler, once the brace was tied in place, was directly in line with and could be seen through the drilled hole. He held it out so Ed could pass judgment. "This going to be alright for the shifter?"

"Sure. Just run the lock nut that's under the glass ball a little up the threads of the gear shift. That should stop the small top end from punching a hole through that there little cloth sack. Should work fine."

From the darkness of it's hideout the cat came slowly forward crouched belly to the floor to inspect the prey it had toppled—to be sure it was safely dead.

"I could fix a thing or two to help you with the pain but you might want something more conventional?"

"I always have some pills in the car for my mother who often has headaches when she rides with me. If it stays bad I may try them."

On the tramp out to Ed's 'top floor suite' he explained, "Reb was a little peeved with us for keeping her up waiting so late. That's why she didn't offer us any sustenance. My fault. She'll get over it."

"We hardly need more tonight or at least I sure don't."

"Glad you qualified that. I never turn her down. She might get to thinking she's not appreciated."

Ed carried a small kerosene 'windproof' lantern in one hand and a roll of blankets under the other arm. He set the lantern on the ground while he leaned forward with the bedroll pinned against the wall to let him use both hands to untwist the wire holding the door shut.

"Got a hook and eye on the inside and you will notice there is one on the outside too and also you might have noticed that little old Buck had that hook lifted when we came along. But he ain't never figured how to untwist a piece of hay wire so that's what I use."

"I'm sure there are any number of latches available that would keep him out."

"Wire's cheap. Free in fact. And easy. Hook that door shut will you. Buck ain't my only problem here. Got to keep Reb's pet deer out too. Hard to understand—we eat venison year round and if we run out—guess who is at the door handing me the gun and shells. Yet, at the same time, she has these pet does with their fawns that would eat us out of house and home given half a chance. They like their little handouts and they know, just like Buck does, where the candy is hidden. There's salt in here too. Let a strange deer come around the yard and Reb will shoot and dress it out all by herself if I ain't home. Makes no sense at all.

"Up there's where we sleep but the elevator ain't working so you got to use the stairway." The 'stairway' was a narrow and perfectly vertical ladder nailed to the edge of the loft floor and extending a bare two feet higher with no other handholds showing.

"I can't get up there with one hand." 'Weak knees and probably a case of vertigo too,' he added under his breath. "I may be feeling better but not that much."

"Shoot yourself. Didn't feel like sharing anyhow. Roll 'em out right here—lots of room." Eddy dropped the blanket roll to the less than clean floor amid the barrels used for grain storage.

"Do I get the lantern?"

"Nope. I got no desire to burn up in the night. It goes with me but I'll set it where it will give you enough light to get beddy by with then it gets blown out. If you need a light through the night just shout out and if you can wake me up I'll light it for you."

The loft floor was low enough that anyone as tall as Ed could have reached up to place the lantern on the edge thereby having both hands free to climb the ladder. But not Ed. Not tonight. Instead, he held the lantern out the full length of his right arm and raced, one handed, up the ladder so fast that it appeared he literally frog-hopped over the short top extension onto the sleeping level ducking at the same time to clear the slope of the roof. He set the lantern near the edge so it gave a bit of light to the lower floor where Reece was rolling out his bed.

"Ah. Reece?"

"What?"

"Might be a good plan to leave an alley way between you and those barrels."

"What for?"

"Well. Traffic gets a little thick down there some nights. Best to leave a clear lane. That way not so many got to run over top of you."

"What traffic?"

147

"You should of been named George. Never ran onto anyone so curious."

"You have rodents in here at night?"

"Hey! Nothing so bad as that. Just a few mice and maybe a rat or two. Reb has the cat tonight so at least there won't be no fighting nor crunching of bones unless my little pet weasel brings in her brood to teach 'em how."

"Weasel! Move that lantern aside."

Ed pulled the lantern back just in time for the bundle of blankets to land where it had been. After some huffing, some shaking of the ladder and of the whole building for that matter, Reece crawled his way around the short top of the ladder and sprawled on the loft floor.

"Made it!"

"How you plan to get back down now?"

"I'll worry about that in the morning."

"You might have to sit on the edge and jump."

"Never mind. Do any of those night creatures ever come up here?

"Aw. They ain't dumb. There's nothing to eat up here 'cept us and I got them pretty much trained to expect a battle."

"You can blow that light out now."

Less than three minutes passed.

"Ed?

No answer.

"I feel a wall of disapproval between us—I mean even beyond what I might deserve for shooting at your horse which I now recognise was a huge tactical error. I think you have misjudged me somewhat."

"Hope so."

"Right now you are steamed up because you have this funny notion I shouldn't look at any woman but Amy and you think I liked your sister too much."

No answer. Reece too was slow to go on as he wondered why he felt the need to explain anything to this kid. "You took

148

me up there on purpose tonight to see how your sister and Percy act toward each other. If we hadn't been invited you still would have found a way to get me to the house. You seem to think I should moon over Amy the same way." Reece pondered the different person the girl, Hettie, had been in the house as compared to her bashful flight from the shop. Inside her own home and in her husband's company she was as confident and competent a hostess as anyone could ask for considering her obviously poor circumstances. "I am not like Percy and Amy is not like your sister—someday you might understand these things better."

"I got eyes."

"Me too and I just couldn't believe what I was seeing"

"Believe."

"I am so intrigued by the women I have seen here today that I find it hard to explain."

"No law says you got to."

"Even so I will try. As it happens, I have only seen four not counting Amy and you would think the law of averages would say two of them would have to be plain looking and one not up to that. Instead, each one has been as much a surprise as the one before until we got to your sister—and she, as you might say yourself, plumb took my breath away."

"I noticed."

"Now don't get stuffy. I'm just trying to explain or to put it plainly, make excuses that I really shouldn't have to make. Maybe it's the long hard road to get here or the rough surroundings and low expectations that make them stand out—surprise factor." 'Or it might simply be the fact that I am still alive,' he added to himself

"More likely it's the hard work and never giving up on the dream of better times. Mending broken plates and broken bones. Washing clothes and darning socks. Packing kids and pushing their men. Not much fun being a woman around these parts. Might be a good thing you didn't look at their hands."

"You shame me."

"Intended to."

"But your sister is so young—seems like she should still be in school—and has no idea yet of the effect she can have on men."

"Right twice—wrong once. She knows. It's a thing she can't help and it's partly why she stays so close to home."

"She should dress differently if she doesn't want men to look at her. At the very least she should pull a paper bag over that cover girl face when strangers come."

"Percy is away at work all week—she tried to look good for him tonight."

"She can't be much older than you are or are you twins?"

"Hey. I'm the senior partner in this generation. I've got nearly three years on Het. Well. More than two."

"No!"

"Like you said, so young she should still be in school. Sweet sixteen and not much more."

Reece blinked rapidly in the darkness. "She seems much too grown up for sixteen."

"Het had to grow up fast."

"Well, I guess so, with two little boys already. The oldest one must be—."

"Whoa now. It's bad enough but not quite that bad. The oldest one is her step son. Percy's by an early wife."

"Ah, yes—Percy—a very lucky man—he certainly made a good choice when he chose to marry her."

"We got two minor little misunderstandings here. One—Het was never Percy's own choice. And two—they ain't married."

Two miles due east—four by road—in Truman Ruff's little house Ruff sat with his head down, elbows on the table and hands over his ears. It was more symbolic than any real effort to block off his hearing because he was listening very closely to every word as his daughter told him about the man she intended to marry if she could. About stepping—inwardly frightened—outwardly bold into his car when he leaned across to open the door for her. She told him about the house on Marine Drive and the apartment too—second prize—and what that meant. Her voice rose with excitement as she described speeding through the rain and darkness with road spray singing past the side window of the Whiskey Six intent on outrunning the Police.

Ruff's heart thudded as to impending disaster.

At Nelson, on the West Arm of Kootenay Lake, the train's scheduled stop was so long that Libby took the opportunity to walk up town until she found a restaurant she liked the look of. She sat with the menu open but mentally counting her money. When the waitress came she ordered coffee with a muffin. Once finished she almost went without leaving a tip—thought of her own hard job and fished in her purse for a nickel to leave.

Chapter 16

"You claim you don't lie so you must be pulling my leg again."

"Not so."

"Percy would have to be blind not to choose her on purpose. I'll bet she's the reason the first wife isn't here."

"Nope. Don't think so. To Percy she was just a kid who lived nearby and was practically never seen. At least not until a month or so after his wife had already left the boy and him to fend for themselves. That's when Het's father—mine too I got to admit— took her up and said to Percy, "here she is, put her to work—put her to bed, she is yours. Or words to that effect."

"I wonder why he would do that."

"Well. I reckon you would have had to work your way into the far corners of his convoluted mind and somehow safely back out again to have any idea why. He did like Percy though. Now that I look at it with eyes in the back of my head I got to admit he might have done right 'cause it seems to have worked out pretty good for both of them."

"You mean 'hindsight'?"

"That's what I said."

"What did your mother think of it?"

"Well now. Old Reb thought the cat said meow. Course the same thing happened to her at about the same age so to her it was just the way it's done—find the poor girl a good man."

"It might not be legal."

The law don't come poking around much out here."

"You didn't like it."

"Well. I reckon I didn't. It's the only thing the old man did in my time that I ever wanted undone. Howsomever—he was nearing death himself by then so it was about the only string he had left to pull and needs to be respected for that."

Outside a small tree limb fell on the roof and rattled till it either came to rest or found a way off. They both listened for more but there were none.

"Reckon it's blowing up top at Hettie's but it's just a breeze down here."

"You talk like you know it all but you're so hopelessly backward and inexperienced that I have to think your head has been in a barrel all these years while you've been growing up."

"That might be so—if this here hill and a few miles around it is the barrel. I ain't been to no city but I do some reading— sometimes stories that happen in cities too."

"You won't get much from reading. You have to get it from real live experience and I would say it's already too late for you."

"I think you been awake so long today that your mind is plumb addled and your tongue unhinged."

Reece breathed deeply for a moment.

"You're hopeless. You need some lessons and I can think of a few I wouldn't mind teaching you."

"Aw. You mean like the one you tried to teach me this afternoon?"

"That was a one time lucky trick you pulled on me. Next time will be different."

"Next time I'll put that first shot an inch lower then we don't got to patch you up and babysit you cause you're so 'sensitive' you got to be handled gentle."

"Your mother didn't really fix anything you know. She just poked and pulled a little—said nothing much was wrong and put this brace on. Anybody could have done that. And speaking of 'next time'—if you get the chance you had better put that first shot more like two inches lower because if you don't you will soon wish you had."

Ed didn't answer. One word kept echoing through his mind in Amy's outraged voice. "Coward!" He could still see her throwing herself between him and Reece. In that one short instant he was shown exactly what she thought of him and where her intentions leaned. A door had closed. 'I wonder how many spare doors I got in there to be fiddled with?' He deeply regretted having fired the shots that had spoiled this day for everyone involved. 'I should have just ridden away.'

"Maybe it was cowardly of me, like Amy said, maybe I should have let you beat me to that pulp you was bragging about. Would that have made you happy?"

"A lot more so than I am now. I wouldn't have hurt you much—I had you so scared that you were already beaten."

Eddy could well agree with that. "What did you mean when you said to Amy that you would deal with her later?"

"Ah, so that's what has been bothering you. You're afraid I'm going to get rough with her are you?" Eddy's reflective mood, the darkness of the night and the almost friendly bantering tone of most of this conversation restored Reece's confidence to where he felt he could now jest with the boy and exact some revenge—at least of a figurative sort. "I meant exactly what I said. The how of it is none of your business. I think I could still beat you to a pulp even with one hand and I've got you cornered here."

"Before you start—just think for a moment about how I can see you in the dark but you can't see me."

There was a long silence

"That was pretty good. I know you're bluffing but now you have me wondering."

"Don't move your head but reach up and scratch the tip of your nose"

"Why?"

"To feel what is waiting there just an inch away."

Reece slowly brought up his good hand toward his nose and just as a finger touched it he was tapped lightly across the knuckles with a substantial feeling club. He jerked his head away and grabbed but all he got was empty air.

"How did you do that?"

"Lie down like a good fellow and I might tell you."

"Okay—how's this?"

"No dice! I said, down. That's better."

"You have some manner of magic night glasses on?"

"Nope. I eat my carrots." He said nothing about the slightly lighter rectangle of the window high above the door that back lighted Reece's profile nicely. "And don't forget, I got my rat swatter here."

"Think you're pretty smart don't you? Probably think your old man raised you the hard way so you are a real tough guy."

"That thought occurred to me once or twice, though 'hard' around here or 'tough' might be different than what you mean."

"If my old man had raised you I doubt you would have lived through it. I nearly didn't a couple of times."

"You prob'ly got what you deserved."

"Oh, I don't mean he slapped me around. Quite different actually. By the time I was your age I was slapping around other people for him. Guys who were slow paying their debts. You beginning to understand?"

"No. What kind of business is your father in?"

"He 'was' in about everything that could turn a quick buck. He was shot four years ago and the 'business' is mine now. Hotels mostly, I've got one that I intend to be the best in town some day and a couple I will probably close down and demolish when they start costing too much."

"You nearly got shot today just like your daddy. You got a kid to take over?"

"No. Maybe I'll will it to you then sit on a cloud and laugh my head off watching you try to ride it."

"Aw. Don't do that. I'd just sell it and blow the money."

"That should be a good show too. What would you blow it on?"

Oh. That's easy. A pickup truck and maybe a good car like that McLaughlin you got out there. Might be a guiding territory I've had my eye on and some more horses."

"With the kind of money I'm talking about you could stand on the hill up at your sister's place and you could pay cash for everything in sight. Then fill it full of horses too if you wanted."

"In that case I s'pose I'd also get a better saddle than what I got now. Maybe even a new one instead of used."

In spite of his scorn, Reece had to laugh.

"But. If I was one of your hotel customers, I reckon I would be a little cautious before going back a second time if getting slapped around was part of the deal."

"Ah, now you are getting closer, 'deal' is a key word here, Ed, at least in the two older joints."

"Oh! Gambling. I was thinking you was in the booze trade what with a car like you got. But it didn't figure with the 'slapping around' cause I thought that would have to be cash on the bottle's cork. Gambling might mean collecting now and then since it might go on credit some but ain't legal either so you can't use the court to do it for you."

"So you do read."

"Aw. Fella just has to watch and listen. We got the same thing goes on here—might be on a smaller scale is all. So you are the bill collector—that must have it's tense moments."

"The tense moments are supposed to be for the collectee. The third time I busted my hand on the other guys jaw the old man bought another car and put me driving on one of his whiskey runs. Lot more dangerous—at least out there where we had competitors pushing to take over who made the cops look like our best friends. But I loved the excitement of it. I loved the car he got for me too—the one that sits outside here tonight. I've kept it for my personal use and the bullet holes you put in it today are not the first to need a patch put over them."

"You still make the whiskey runs do you? Around here we call it rum running but I guess it's all the same."

"Sure, but I'm not in that any more, nor the gambling either. Those things still go on of course and things happen in hotels that make money for me but I don't have to lift a finger for them since I took over when Dad got killed."

"You don't worry that the same thing will happen to you some day or some dark night?"

"Not as much as he should have because, as I have been trying to tell you, I am right out of all the risky parts of it now. By ultimatum more than by choice I have to admit."

"Cops find out who did it?"

"There was no question about who did it but in the long run it went across as a hunting accident so there was no one charged. The Police didn't care a lot—one down—one less to go."

"But. Something tells me the former 'collector' cared. Did it end there?"

"It ended in a burned out car a hundred feet below a sharp corner."

"Um. And I suspect the former 'collector' busted his hand and sprained his wrist about then."

"He did not. The guy had a broken neck—different technique."

"Did the Police care about that one?"

"They tried to blame it on me but failed."

"I reckon I'm glad enough. If the law couldn't touch him somebody had to get it done."

"You surprise me."

"Me—I'd of thought the same way—on that."

"Just the same, they tried to nail me for my father's killing and if it weren't for some gaps in their so called evidence, they might have made a case of it."

"Were you in the hunting party?"

"I was home running the show while the old man was hunting north of Kamloops but they tried to prove that I paid for it."

"But you didn't."

"No. For a while it looked like the end for me too because the people who did arrange it were pretty big so I was under pressure from both sides. I had to pull in my horns and let them have what they wanted although they paid well for it once they found I was agreeable and wouldn't make waves. After that was settled they let me have my revenge. Now I am nothing more than a hotel owner."

"I reckon I kind of like things plain and simple like it is here."

"Depends on what you grow up to I guess."

Both were quiet so long that each began thinking the other was asleep at last. The rustle and scurry of small feet down below around the grain barrels became the loudest noise in the building.

"Where does Amy fit into all this?"

Reece found himself strangely comfortable with the question. "That's for her to decide."

"Actually, I reckon she already has. Just wondered about you."

"Her and I—we think alike, Ed. She's the only girl I have ever found with such nerve. You should see her when the cops are close behind with their siren going and lights flashing—sharp corners coming into the headlight beams up front. Maybe we'll go splat against a tree or a rock some night with the cops chasing us but I don't really think so. She lives for excitement and danger just like I do but I expect we will live long enough to slow down."

"Thought you didn't do the night runs anymore."

"I don't. But it sure is fun to buzz a cop, let him think for a while that he can catch me and then show him that he can't."

"Well, I reckon you are right, Reece. I am just a dumb cowboy who smells like his horse." And then to himself, 'also, I am sorry about all my bad thoughts toward you—my mistake.' But it was not a thing he would ever say out loud. At least not without a lot of thought on how to say it.

Still at Nelson, the train sat waiting so long that Libby's pretended sleep, despite the coffee, became so real that she did not awaken when at two A.M.- a few minutes later than the schedule advertised—it finally began moving. Three hours along the way when she did stir and sit up the new day had already started to push and heave last night on over the next range of mountains to the west. The train was climbing high on a hillside with a faint suggestion of water and flat land below in the shadows as they slowed for yet another stop. Two grain elevators told her where she was and the name on the station confirmed it—Creston. Only five more hours to Elko.

Chapter 17

S ure footed little Buck was falling. Going down so sudden Eddy had no time to swing clear. The ground was coming up fast and he knew it was going to hurt.

"That dream again," he breathed in relief not sitting fully up this time, "nothing but the dream." Still, as if it were a scripted part of his day, he rubbed his left cheek where it seemed to smart from contact with the ground. There was no feel of blood or injury so he eased back down hoping to sleep some more. His left ankle hurt too until he flexed it a few times.

It was becoming more real each time! And not a stumble that might be corrected but rather the free fall of four legs that no longer worked—neck outstretched—chin plowing into the dirt then turning under.

There had been a sound too. A crack of thunder?

'Well, little Buck. Might be you and me better stay at home today.'

But it was only a dream.

Eddy raised up enough to look over the sleeping Reece at the window where he could faintly make out the shape of the nearest trees beyond the corral—morning almost here. Quietly

he slipped out of his blankets and with the 'rat swatter' tight in
his right hand eased himself over Reece's legs.

When Reece awoke it was daylight and he found that Eddy
had managed to crawl over him and down the ladder without
disturbing his sleep. One handed it was no easier getting down
the ladder than getting up had been but he did it rather than jump
and possibly jar his sore hand. No one was in sight when he
eased the door open—at least Ed hadn't wired it shut from outside. He was glad to see the car parked yet just as it had been last
night. It wouldn't have surprised him to find the kid had driven
off someplace with it. Ten miles or so to the east, the sun had just
cleared the mountain top horizon.

"Bout time you showed up. Could of had half my day's work
done by now if it weren't I had to baby sit you. City livin' teach
you all these lazy, slacker habits?"

Ed, wearing a heavy coat against the morning chill was seated on another, older looking jacket draped over a stump so near
the corral that the rails served as a back rest for him. Now he
rose as though, indeed, he had been waiting for nothing else but
Reece's appearance.

"Never mind your lip, Kid. I'll be gone as fast as I can get
my car running and turned around." The sight of Ed with his
rifle propped against the fence beside him stirred all the animos-
ity that Reece had felt for him yesterday—to think this skinny
joker had the gall to walk with Amy! 'I talked too much last
night,' he admitted to himself. It must have been because the
kid had tricked him so neatly and gained the upper hand. Last
night's need to brag—to regain 'face'—now seen in the cool
light of dawn, seemed a childish thing to have done—and dangerous too—Eddy might think he could make trouble now. Let
him try!

The kid was surprisingly perceptive though—so much so that
Reece feared he might have guessed at things beyond what were
said. For instance that he—the son with too much of his moth-

er's kind nature—was nothing at all like the father he liked to brag about had been. While the old man lived and ruled, the son had swaggered and blustered and with his wrist brace and brass knuckles kept the minions in alignment while the father made the deals that swelled the bank accounts. Even with the old man gone and everything but the legitimate parts of the business gone with him, Reece had never quit pretending that he still headed the same organisation. 'And now I wonder why I bothered. Eddy doesn't pretend to be more than just what he is—quite the opposite—he takes every opportunity to pass himself off as a dumb cowboy working hard at being no more than just that.'

For the first time he admitted that he was glad the old shady deals stuff was gone. As for the 'accident' to his father's killer—well—real accidents do happen and necks sometimes get broken in rollovers and long falls down to the rocks. The kid had seemed to believe and approve of the story spun to him and Reece guessed that could mean that Eddy, despite his youth and inexperience—or perhaps because of it—just might be the tougher minded of the two. And he didn't care one little bit! He just wanted to see the last of this kid in his too big pants.

"Hey! You aiming to pull your freight without going in to thank old Reb for all the help she gave you? Free? You won't get that kind of fixing in no city."

"All that mumbo jumbo did was to make it hurt worse than ever this morning." But he turned to the house knowing Ed was right. He owed a thank you to the woman who had been so considerate and helpful even if her treatment was as crude as crude could be. He knocked at the door but heard no response.

"Don't be bashful, Rum Runner, walk right on in, she ain't used to knocks on her door."

Gritting his teeth Reece opened the door, stepped inside and called out, "good morning Mrs.—". He couldn't remember the name and had almost said, 'Stuart' the daughters name. But it didn't matter because the place was so small that by now he knew it was empty. He stormed back out leaving the door open behind him.

Ed was sitting yet on the coat covered stump but now the rifle lay across his knees.

"She's not home!"

"Course not. You don't think she's going to sit around all day waiting like I been doing—not with a whole day of work ahead of her and Hettie."

"You stinking little rat! You weasel faced, two bit, imitation cowboy! I've a notion to rub your face all over this hillside."

"Thoughtful of you old friend. But was I you, I wouldn't bother." Ed shifted the rifle a bit to the charging Reece who saw his error and swerved away toward the car.

"I'll pass on your kind and sincere message of gratitude to old Reb when she gets home and she truly will be glad to get it. In the meantime, the faster you pour your carcass into that fine automobile and make dust out of here the sooner we both will smile. Sorry about no breakfast but the cook couldn't wait. Reckon Ruffs' will feed you. You should find your way as long as you take a left when you hit the main road and another left at the first junction."

"If we ever meet again, Kid, you had better see me first."

"I'm sure I will."

Reece must have found his hand brace quite satisfactory for shifting gears because once he had the shift lever modified to fit he was quickly turned around and on his way. On impulse Ed extended his right hand shoulder high, palm open as the car, on a final swing, made it around to the way out. Reece was scowling but at that same instant, moved his injured hand across to as similar a gesture as he could manage. Twenty feet farther along the car halted abruptly and after a moment for gear changing backed close enough to Ed that Reece could speak without raising his voice. "Well, my friend, if we ever do meet again I want you on my side. And please do tell your mother thank you for me. I shall indeed think well of her from time to time."

Ed sat quite a while wondering about that enigmatic and spontaneous lifting of the hands almost as if there had been a rubber band connection. "Aw. I reckon I might have survived the skirmish but he has won the battle and I was plain and simple admitting it and wishing him good luck. Don't know what he was wishing—might be that he hadn't shot at Buck."

Buck, listening with just one ear, flicked the other forward too at mention of his name.

Ed's thoughts went quiet, 'I reckon that wave which likely neither one of us will ever be able to explain was what triggered his notion to back up and deliver a civil and welcome message. Reckon I finally saw the real man right there—too bad we met under such—um—'trying' circumstances.'

'All that silly bravado last night and this morning—that's not me—that's a looser trying to starch up his backbone and convince himself the booby prize was just what he really wanted all along. But I was plumb wrong about Amy 'cause it's plain as day she sure ain't my type! Kind of rhymes with grapes that ain't ripe. Reckon I know now where the word 'sarcastic' comes from 'cause this stuff sure enough tastes sour and caustic.'

"Well, Buck, seeing as you ain't saddled yourself I reckon I will have to do it for you and then we'll lope over to the 'Pine' and see if old Ruff is getting anything done without us. As for girls! Well. Might be the smart thing to do is to sit back and wait for Chuck and Myrtle's little girls to grow up and see if one turns out like her Ma." On that, the first cheerful thought of the day, he shrugged out of his coat, picked up the extra one and headed for the shed to trade them for the saddle.

At Lumberton, a family and three men got off from Libby's coach but more got on than got off so she found herself having to share her seat with an elderly couple. She didn't mind though once she learned they were only on for the twenty something minute run to Cranbrook. This ride gave them most of the day to shop before catching the west bound train back home late in the afternoon. They prattled on about their two sons, such a pity, neither had found a common sense girl to marry yet. They made good money working in the sawmill as did the one—Libby missed whether he was son or son in law—who worked out in the woods. She was highly amused when she realised they were suggesting that she come visit sometime to meet their sons. In spite of her tiredness she sat up straighter and surreptitiously tried to make herself less rumpled. She almost missed them when they got off at Cranbrook along with nearly everyone else in the coach.

At least the diversion had taken her mind off her own worries for a little while. It had been nice to talk with people who's biggest trouble seemed to be that they had sons who were still single. She fretted now that Truman might not be picking up his mail promptly—might be letting it pile up for a week at a time. There might be no one to meet her at the Elko station. That would be a major disaster for while she had enough to buy her return ticket if it was needed, there was no extra money for hiring a ride or staying over. She was most definitely not going to walk the Sheep Mountain trail as some people from south of the Elk River did even if it was a lot shorter than the road.

Less than two more hours.

Ruff sat alone at his table with a half full cup of stale and cold coffee close to one hand. Every once in a while he raised it, barely touched the bitter brew to his lips then put it down exactly in it's sticky circle on the table. Everything was moving much too fast for him. So few days since Libby's warning letter had come. And the telegram yesterday—too late—the man was here ahead of it or at least ahead of it being read.

It was too much! The long struggle to make a farm of this place. Others managed to make hay land of their properties though it has to be admitted that the successful ones all had a reliable source of water. That's what the ditch is for but it has taken so long. So many setbacks requiring him to shelve the project and take a job away from home. Home for all of them one time. Amy was six months old when they came here and lived in a tent while Libby helped him build the house. They didn't buy the land, they just took it and called it theirs. Then came the failed effort to siphon water from the lake over the ridge—so embarrassing to sink so much time and hope into it and then discover the lake was too low in elevation for it to work. Too many busybody's asking about the land—"Doesn't show as surveyed on the map—how did you come to own it?" Questions, questions and more questions. They couldn't leave it alone so, in self defence, he went to the Government Office where he discovered it was quite easy to file a claim on it so he did that.

But that set a process into motion. A process geared to a fixed schedule. Timed steps by which he must show progress or at the end of five years he could be evicted. Being here as a squatter with no legal right but at the same time no pressure to perform had been better.

And then the bickering with Libby, she was fed up and after so much time and work invested in it she wanted to leave. She wanted him to work at a sawmill instead. When he tried to explain that they would loose the farm if he did that, she shouted, "GOOD" then added insult, "What farm? You mean this pile of gravel?" When the dust settled from that Libby and Amy were gone. Then, with her not here to carp at him, he did what she had wanted and went to work in the woods. At first he had to bunk away from home so time passed with little gain on any front. Simon succeeded in getting water piped to his sawmill and that blew new hope into Ruff's water scheme so Ruff went to work for him. He lived at home but ate at the cookhouse rather than make his own meals. A new cook came to work for Simon but Ruff hardly noticed until one day he suddenly understood that she was nursing a loss of her own. He fell then for Corrie who was lonely and fell for him. He spent a lot of time in the back room at the cookhouse where Errol was now spending a lot of time. Errol, who along with his brother, is hanging like a vulture on an updraft waiting to get water from the ditch for their own land.

Libby sued for a divorce and got it. Now their precious only child has gone off with the very same man Libby says is a criminal to meet her at the train and bring her here later today.

He banged his fist on the table, "How much can a man stand? HOW MUCH?" He looked at his rifle on the wall and longed for the nerve to put the barrel in his mouth and hook a thumb on the trigger. 'NO! NEVER! With my success rate I'd blow the teeth out one side of my mouth and be lying here in a pool of blood but still alive when they got home. Amy was right—I should leave this place of failure and go somewhere else.'

"If only I could!"

Then there was that stupid, know it all Indian kid who said he wasn't Indian. 'He turned me into a thief and with Amy's help has made me a booze smuggler as well!'

'We did get a lot of work done though and done quickly too. When he is around I work harder and more efficiently. He looks so funny in those pants that are half again too big. If there is one last thing I do around here I must buy him a pair that fit.'

'I can't buy anything.'

'I'll steal a pair that fit! I'll break into the store and steal a pair and that will be poetic justice. Better yet—I will stuff that filthy fifty dollars the Rum Runner gave me into a pocket of those new pants.' Having finally remembered the envelope inside his shirt he now dug it out—found a pencil and printed Eddy's name on it. A moment later he added—'thanks,'—then the initials of the man who had given it to him. After more thought he folded the envelope to fit into the nearly empty coffee can and put it back in it's place. Amy never made coffee unless he asked for it so it should be safe there until he had the new pants to put it in.

He was still sitting there imagining the kid in stolen pants that fit when he heard a horse arriving and he knew without looking that it would be Eddy coming to find out why he wasn't at work on the ditch. This added aggravation when, with just a hundred yards or two to go, he knew in his heart that the project had ended.

"Only so much Lord! Please. Only so much."

Chapter 18

"Well. He ain't here, Buck. What do you suppose is goin' on that is more important to him than this here water ditch? Wonder if that snake in the grass, Reece, has anything to do with this?"

Ed rode along the intended route of the last connecting portion of the ditch but found no sign of the man or his tools. Only the broken branches that Ed had pushed into the ground every thirty or forty feet to indicate the exact route the water would need to follow were to be seen. Ruff had been a little scornful of Ed's need for stakes to show the way—he would have eyeballed it. However, with the evidence of his own drastic and time consuming error just a few feet away on the down slope side, he had refrained from excessive comment.

"How about that! Reckon we better ride down and see what's wrong. First though, I reckon we might as well run back to the post office and get the rest of yesterday's mail. Should be there to pick up by now and old Ruff seems to like getting it before it goes stale." Buck agreed—you could tell by the flick of ears and the toss of head.

As uncomplimentary as Errol could be about people who did not meet his approval he always seemed genuinely pleasant and respectful to Eddy. Since the boy had started helping Ruff and picking up the man's mail there had been no derogatory comments about the ditch digger either. "Sorry about the interruption yesterday, Eddy. Got it all here now but there's not much more." He handed over the paper Ruff had complained about the absence of and one large letter size envelope. Ed thought there was something odd in the way Errol handed over the letter—as though he would rather hold it back but couldn't since it was 'mail' and must not be tampered with. But Errol's cheerful manner overrode the impression of 'hanging onto' so Ed dismissed the notion as imagined.

"How's the grand canal project proceeding? Getting along toward finished?"

"It is. Still got to see Mike over at the barns about borrowing a team and that big walking plough they use for making sidehill cuts when they build logging road. A few minutes with that and old Ruff can start shovelling water. Looks like it should run free right on down to his place."

"Good, good, glad to hear it. It's been a long slow job, nice to see it nearing the end."

Errol spoke as though he too had been out there working his fingers raw and showed a certain small hint of ownership that Ed did not like. But it wasn't for him to argue, his sole interest was in helping Ruff get it finished and then it would be 'so long, John'. Whether he had wanted to help because Ruff was Amy's father or because the man so plainly needed help to save him from himself was still open to negotiation. A few days ago it might have been the former but now, since yesterday, more likely to be the later.

A car purred past outside leaving such a cloud of dust in it's wake that rushing to the window left Ed no wiser since the machine was lost to view. The route that the road wound through the mill and camp meant it would soon be climbing into sight on the hillside where the road turned up a draw on its way to the main highway. Ed watched there until it passed into the draw.

Reece's car alright but sun glint on the side windows made it impossible to tell if he was alone or not. He might have dropped Ruff off at the ditch.

"Got to go, Errol, might be back on my regular wood detail in a day or two so I'll be seeing you and Floyd at the cookshack again."

"Good show, Ed, see you then."

Back at the ditch line there was still no Ruff so Ed, carrying the mail, cut a bee line for the house taking the cow trail route that Ruff always used.

He made no effort to approach the place quietly being quite sure that Reece was gone and if not—let the chips fall. The man had seemed friendly enough a few hours ago but, "if he finds me around Amy he might not be so happy." Eddy dropped Buck's reins by the porch step and as he crossed to the door, called out, "hello this house."

From within came a muttered reply. "Door's not locked."

Ed closed the door after entering then pulled out a chair for himself and settled down across from Ruff who sat there looking like a thundercloud fresh out of rain and lightning.

"You all alone?"

"As alone as any man can ever be. Feel free to pull out a chair and sit down. Seeing as you already have."

"Thanks Ruff. Where is Amy?"

"Gone."

"Where to?"

"Physically? To Elko. Truly and for ever? She is gone to Hell with that thug who came and got her."

"Reece?"

"I guess that's his name. Tall guy, one bad hand. Big black car with a busted headlamp."

"Why to Elko?"

"To meet the train. It should be me going to meet it but my car is out of gasoline."

"Why does the train need to be met?"

"Libby is coming on it—Amy's mother. She warned me, she told me to shoot him and I didn't. There is my gun on the wall—loaded even—and I let them go."

"Hey! That's strong talk, Ruff. You can't just up and shoot at people you know. You might hurt somebody."

"I shoot rats—you shoot rats—but I let this one get away. He'll be back though, I might get up the nerve yet."

"Now. Cool off some. You got no call to take it so hard. Sure, she is your daughter and your only kid to boot but girls do grow up and get to wanting to live their own life just like the rest of us you know. And it don't matter if you like him or not a man has to come from somewhere to help that come about. Just 'cause you know nothing about him don't mean he's not the right one for her."

"That's the trouble. I know way too much about him. Libby warned me but I was too busy working to pay the attention to it that I should've. He snuck in here and while I was trying to grasp what was happening he stole Amy and took her away. Now Libby is coming but she is too late too."

"Maybe you should clue me in on what all this guy is supposed to have done."

"Done? He's a killer, Ed. He hired a man to kill his own father so he could get the money and hotels the old man owned. Then he killed the hit man to keep him from talking. He smuggles booze and Lord knows what else. He sells 'protection'—you must know what I mean—to all the smaller dealers he sells to and he buys protection for them all from the law. He's into crooked gambling and the cops never touch him so you figure that one out. And I lacked the guts to shoot him! Just because he was so darned polite."

"Hey, man! Tone it down. You are talking about a good friend of mine and I wish you would look for the truth before you accuse him of things he didn't do. Who told you all this wild stuff about him?"

Ruff would never admit that Amy's long and too detailed declaration of intent plus his own imagination had merely fuelled the flames that Libby had lit. Besides, the man does drive a McLaughlin. "You don't know this guy, Ed, you've no place in your honest and simple mind to understand the evils he deals in every day." The irony of referring to Eddy as 'honest' occurred to Ruff but he dismissed it as a matter of relativity.

"You got that both right and wrong. There's things happen in this old world that I ain't got a pigeon hole for but Reece ain't a guy that falls outside the loop."

"You don't know anything about him. If you knew everything Amy has told me while at the same time pretending that none of it happens anymore, you might well have shot him yourself."

"Hey! I don't run around shooting people for no reason at all. 'Specially a man I know so well that I both like and respect him like a brother."

"How d'you happen to know him so well?"

"Well! Didn't he eat at Reb's table last night? Him and me sitting together?"

"I didn't know that."

"Aw. You should of guessed. You got no guest room around here so he went and stayed the night with us. Him and me, we went up and visited with Hettie and Percy and their little boys and we all plumb enjoyed the evening. Besides that he shared my room to sleep in and we lay awake three quarters of the night talking about when we was kids. We got so much in common that it's plumb a wonder we can bear to part now we finally found each other. I know for dead certain, Ruff, that he did not kill his father. He loved his old man just as I loved mine. He was a delicate and sensitive kid as he grew up and there wasn't much he could do without messing up. His kind hearted old father put up with him anyway and kept finding easier jobs for him. The man who shot his father did it 'cause he expected to gain for himself and the accident that caught up to him later was no more than rough justice well served."

"As for all those other far fetched notions you were yapping about—forget it—it ain't so. Sure. He owns hotels but it's an honourable trade and besides that, other people run them for him 'cause no man could keep up to so much all by himself. Hotels have rooms in which things happen of which he has no knowledge and over which he has no control. That's just the hotel business for you. The law says you can't turn people away if they need shelter and have the money to pay for a room. So then some guys get a few games of chance going in a rented space and some make money and some loose. Is the owner—who is not actually connected to the business of running the place— somehow supposed to know about it and go shut them down and throw them out? I kind of doubt it. The same thing happens right here wherever men live in bunkhouses. It happens at farmhouse kitchen tables too though the stakes there might be match sticks 'cause nobody has any money."

"That's different. I don't think you know what you are talking about."

"And why is it different? Is it 'cause nobody tells you about it so it don't count?"

"Small stakes, Ed, nobody gets hurt."

"Aw. You know as well as I do that there's games right there in Simon's camp that clean out a months pay from half the crew and put it in the pockets of two or three who are a little better than average with the cards. Does that count?"

"We're getting away from the main issue here."

'Yeah. We are. The main issue is that your daughter—your only child—is standing at a fork in the road of her life. The man she has chosen has her by the hand but she is looking back at you and her mother."

"What d'you mean by that?"

"I mean the next move is yours, you can wave goodbye and she leads him down one fork. Or you can turn your back and they go down the other one."

"Do I dare ask what the difference is?"

"Sure. If you wave goodbye the road she takes will wind around and every once in a while will come back alongside yours. The other one, if you turn your back, goes straight away and you never see her again."

Ruff shook his head like a wounded bear. "It's too much for me, Eddy, it's coming at me from all sides. I'm going to have to break something so I can throw the pieces and this crook is what I want to break."

"Ruff. I tell you he is no crook. I spent a night lying three feet from him and talking in the dark about most everything before we went to sleep. You don't do that without finding out if a man can be trusted. No matter what he might say in the give and take and brag of conversation, you can't help but come around to understanding how he thinks. The feeling I get for this guy is that he is a good man who will treat Amy well. I reckon his biggest faults are simple enough—his temper is a bit quick—like yours—and his foot is a little heavy on the gas pedal. Here, open your mail and calm down. Your paper has come so you can read up on whatever schemes and dreams Fernie council is pushing now."

"What's this letter? From the 'Province of British Columbia' it says, 'Water Branch'. Why would they write to me?"

"Prob'ly the bill for your water rights to Mountain Creek where the pipeline comes from."

"Better not be! I've never applied for water rights and I don't intend to until I prove to myself that I can get it here. I'm not going to pay for something I haven't—."

Ruff went silent as he read the enclosure from the official looking envelope. His face had been flushed, now it went so dark red that it became almost black as his eyes bulged and his jaw hung slack. He let out a bellow that may have been intended to convey some meaning but instead came out as an animal roar of rage. He lurched up with such a sudden lunge that he sent the table against Eddy knocking him and his chair over with the table landing on top pinning him down.

"THAT DOES IT! I'LL KILL THEM BOTH! AND I'LL KILL HER TOO!"

Clumsily, as if half dazed, he wadded the paper in his hands, threw it against the wall then reached for his rifle. By then Ed had crawled out from under the overturned table and he stood in Ruff's way.

"Whoa man. Let's talk this over. Let me read tha- "

That was the instant Ruff's right fist plowed into Eddy just above the belt buckle lifting him completely off the floor and landing him atop the remains of the chair he had already smashed when the table took him over.

For Eddy, it was a new discovery, a world in which there was no air. None left inside to expel to get things working again and none outside able to rush into the vacuum that was his lungs. He gasped for a breath that would not come then collapsed sideways quite unconscious.

For Ruff, it was a satisfactory if not exactly an intentional outcome. "There," he growled, "maybe that will keep you out of trouble while I take care of this business."

Chapter 19

Libby crowded the trainman as they slowed for Elko. He had opened the door and raised the iron plate that covered the steps now he braced himself to hold her from pushing him off the train as she crowded against him straining for a look at the people waiting on the platform. But he was tolerant. 'Must be nice to get home,' he thought, 'she must have been away a long time.'

As she willed the train to stop the first familiar face she saw was Amy. Thank Goodness she is here. Where is Truman? Still standing on the coach steps where she had the advantage of height to scan the small crowd she became a road block to those wanting off from behind her. Her eyes, which had denied what they saw and kept up the search for someone else, returned reluctantly to the man beside Amy. One look at the way they moved forward together and she knew. Too late! Ruff has failed. Again.

The trainman had to reach for her arm and urge her to take the last step down for she had become frozen in place. He never tired of watching the high emotions of passengers and those who met them. It was always better than the sometimes tragic partings that he also saw every week or two at one stop or another.

177

This attractive woman is well met and he felt a vicarious thrill of homecoming for her.

Libby walked to meet them like any glad mother might but her eyes saw Amy alone and cut the man with her right out of the picture. Her daughter hugged her but she did not respond. Reece tried to take her suitcase but she turned her back to him and her death like grip on it could not be broken. He gave up in disgust and let her carry it to the car. She came to life at the side of the McLaughlin but still ignoring him, she spoke to Amy instead. "No! I might as well stay here and catch the next train west."

"Please, Mother, come home with us for a few days and talk to Father, he needs you."

"Is Tru there? At home?"

"Yes, he is and times have been very hard for him."

"Times will always be hard for that man. Where is—she?"

"Corrie has not been home since I got here. I think that's all over with. Father might even be ready to finally give up on that impossible place. He was so distraught when we left—so worried about so many things—that I fear what he might think up to do. If there is any one person who can talk him out of it and into leaving it will be you."

Libby sighed and let the suitcase go as Reece pried at her fingers again. "I can't ride there!" She snapped it out like a drill sergeant as he opened the back door for her. Reece, taken by surprise looked to Amy who also seemed a little stunned.

"That's right, I had forgotten, she gets carsick in the back—she has to ride in front."

Reece rolled his eyes but opened the front door instead and Libby climbed in as though she now could not be kept out. He closed the door a little harder than necessary but smiled when Amy squeezed his hand as she got into the back seat. He shut her door more gently then went around to the driver's side, stowed the suitcase on the floor in back next to Amy's feet and climbed in behind the steering wheel. Libby shifted a little sideways so she didn't have to acknowledge his presence.

By the time they slewed around the 'S' turns of the sand trap and up the hill to the north end of Long Prairie alongside the Great Northern tracks both Amy and her mother knew they were in for the ride of their lives.

Eddy came awake slowly. The first sound he heard seemed to be that of a pump working somewhere—thumping along steadily. He was mildly surprised to discover it was his own heart. Next he heard someone breathing—deep, slow and comfortably—it felt so close and so good that he decided that too must be himself. The sound of a clock came from somewhere inserting it's noisy ticking into the scene but time meant nothing to him right now. He was just happy to lie here in peace with his eyes closed.

"Ruff! Where is he?" The cry in his mind was just loud enough to bring his eyes open and then he couldn't place himself—this is not where he normally awakened. The crumpled pages of paper in front of him brought it back and brought him upright. "Ruff hit me. Did he ever hit me!"

He scrambled to his feet finding he was quite alright—just a little sore in the midsection. He must have lain out cold for some time—long enough for his breath to come back to normal.

"I won't laugh again at Reece for fainting."

Eddy went to the open door and out onto the porch. Buck was there just twenty feet away pretending he had found some grass to nibble. Lucky Ruff was not a horseman.

Who was he going to kill?

"Both of them and her too!"

"Who was 'them'—Amy and Reece? Then her mother too? Which way did he go and how long ago?"

Eddy rushed back into the house and scooped up the crumpled letter that had caused Ruff's explosion—spread it out carefully to avoid tearing any of it—skipped over the headings that indicated it had come from the Water Rights Branch and read—

Mr. Truman Ruff:

It has been brought to my attention that you are planning to make use of water from Mountain Creek south of Elko in Kootenay Land District. Also, that your plans include making use of a works and/or diversion constructed by a currently licensed user.

It is my duty to inform you that this stream (Mountain Creek) is now fully committed and if you are found to be taking water from this stream (Mountain Creek) you will be prosecuted to the full extent of the law.

Below is a list of licensed users of this stream (Mountain Creek).

There was more, and a signature too, but Ed skipped to the handful of listed and therefore licensed users. Only the last two caught his interest.

Errol N. Fuller
Floyd G. Fuller
Named as owner/operators of Fuller Ranches.
And something about acre feet.

There were pages with drawings of said licensed works and diversions with one whole page for the diversion by the Brothers' Fuller. It was drawn up before Ruff had seen the need for the flume but otherwise was a fairly accurate drawing of the existing pipe as laid in Ruff's ditch line by Simon and of the ditch now being constructed by Ruff and Eddy.

Eddy carefully folded the pages as one, tucked them into a shirt pocket and buttoned the flap. He pulled out the big pocket watch—wondered for a moment about the dead man who had one time gone through the same motions with it—then put it away without noting or caring what time it was.

"I am shilly shallying while I decide how much of a coward I am. The trail home sure does look mighty good right now."

Buck lifted his head and snorted.

Eddy walked to him and stood, cheek to bigger cheek, rubbing ears and neck.

"Let's go little Buck, there's a job to do and I reckon I need your help. Old Ruff, who has become a good friend of ours is in big trouble—we got to go and save him from himself. Might be it'll not turn out so bad."

They did not tear up the valley at full gallop like Buck wanted to do for Ed was still undecided. He had no idea how long he had lain unconscious on the kitchen floor—it might be all over by now. Or Ruff may have come to his senses and be stopped to mull it over—sounds of fast pursuit might send him raging again. For sure, a tumble because of a careless speeding hoof in a gopher or badger hole wouldn't help anyone. All he knew for certain was that Ruff would not be following the road. He would be travelling the cattle trail that paralleled it just as he always did—just as Eddy always did because it was less dusty and more shaded.

They jumped and spooked a small band of wild horses coming from the west who raced away to the north with manes and tails flying. With them went any hope of surprising Ruff. 'On the other hand,' Eddy thought, 'with them running past, he might not look back at one more horse coming from behind.'

It presented an opportunity.

Eddy slacked the reins to let Buck pick the pace and it became very fast. The little buckskin took the wild bunch as a challenge and worked hard to keep up or even to pass and head them off. Halfway to the mill the wild ones veered suddenly to the right and Buck wanted to follow but Eddy kept him going straight ahead because the abrupt change in course must mean the front runners had seen Ruff.

Eddy saw him too—his dirty blue shirt a splash of alien colour amid the trees. Not a fast walker and certainly never a runner, his stolid steady stride nonetheless carried him over rough ground as if it were flat and smooth. There would be no reasoning with him—Eddy had found that out already. No point in calling to him and probably getting shot along with the three at the mill plus whoever else got in the way. Here is where he should dismount and shoot the man from behind before he became aware that he was being caught up to and could begin his own incredibly accurate fire.

Trade the death of one for the life of three.

'A hard thing to do. My gun may not want to.'

'No more so than me.'

There didn't seem to be any other quick and easy options though—to shoot a leg with high velocity, soft nose hunting ammunition could be the same as blowing it off with dynamite. To hit the shoulder might kill with the shock of shattered bones. Ruff's erratic movement ruled out any attempts at fancy shots to take the rifle from his hands. Besides, being desperate, afraid, and reluctant is no substitute for being angry. Without spontaneity the bullet may refuse to fly true.

There was a better way that might work and the wild horses still running close to one side were the key to make it possible. Ride him down! Run Buck right over top and break him up without killing him and leave him some chance to recover. Buck won't want to do it—he will try to swerve. Eddy tightened his knees, shortened his grip on the reins so his hand was snug to the mane, hoped the little horse would understand and prepared to guide him to the point of impact.

But even with the noise of the horse herd running past, Ruff picked out the extra hoof beats behind and swung to face Eddy and Buck—swung the rifle too. Eddy saw fire in the barrel behind the shadowed streak of bullet. Between his knees he felt a part of Buck turn to mush inside.

Sure footed little Buck was falling. Going down so sudden that Eddy had no time to swing clear. The ground was coming up fast and he knew it was going to hurt. This was not the dream—he would not wake up, rub his cheek and go back to sleep. This was the free fall of four legs that no longer reached ahead to the next step. Buck's chin plowed into the dirt, skidded a ways then head and neck turned under as hind quarters rose high into the air with the momentum of forward travel.

His dismount incomplete but at least free of the stirrups, Ed hit the ground in front of his somersaulting horse. As he rolled he saw Buck standing neatly, impossibly, on his nose. Time stood still as he scrambled to get clear of those hundreds of pounds coming down at him. Everything he did was so slow and Buck, after that instant of hanging in place, was coming down on him so fast. At the last instant he turned his feet flat sideways to the ground so they would not be caught heels up, toes down. It hurt anyway as both feet were caught under the fallen horse. There was a bounce and Eddy jerked enough to have one foot free before everything settled and stilled.

It seemed a long time that he lay there half stunned but when he lifted his head to look around the dust was still settling over him and Buck. He spit dirt from his mouth, saw it was bloody and spit again. His face felt numb so he brushed fingers along his cheek and they came away red and wet with blood. Both Ed and Buck now faced back to where they had come from with Ed's left foot pinned under the horse. He put his right foot against the saddle and pushed as he pulled with his left but he was stuck tight.

Buck began kicking his hind feet almost in a running motion then the front feet too. He lurched as if trying to get up nearly freeing Ed's foot before the movements became totally uncoordinated and even dangerous to the trapped boy.

"Buck! You are a dead horse running. Lie still!"

The movements subsided but did not stop. Eddy became afraid that now, having survived the fall, he was going to be trampled or rolled on by his dying horse. Twisting and stretching he was just able to reach his saddle gun and pull it free. Levering in a cartridge he shot Buck where spine became skull and at last all movement ceased.

"Buck! Damn!"

Reece knew the road now, at least a lot better than when he had made his first trip southward from Elko yesterday. Was it only yesterday? Now he knew at what speed he could take the hairpin turn at the edge of the void where the road dived into the canyon. He used that knowledge to sail over the last rise at a speed that left stomachs hanging in mid air to catch up only when the wheels came back firmly to the road surface. Braking smoothly and shifting down he could only hope that no one was coming up the hill. He took the corner sliding outward on loose gravel but hit the throttle—cranked the wheel and powered his way back to the driving tracks.

Shifted to high gear again the McLaughlin went into free fall down the nearly straight but steep and narrow road. Amy was ecstatic—it showed in her eyes and her grin. Libby was a statue—refusing to show fear though her right leg was strangely stiffened since, while she did not drive, she knew very well which foot pushed on the brake. It was a battle of wills, Amy watched Reece exact revenge for her mother's contempt of him and laughed, she hadn't had so much fun since being sent home to her father.

But Reece's thoughts veered suddenly, 'What on earth am I doing? Eddy wouldn't do this! Certainly, he can be a showoff too as he proved when he climbed the ladder to the sleeping loft one handed last night—but he would never terrorize a woman as I am doing now to Amy's mother.' His foot went to the brake pedal. It didn't help matters any either that there were no objections from the daughter—'she has ridden with me enough that she has faith that all will end well.' He visualised the brake bands closing on the fast spinning drums and heat beginning to build. 'I hope that faith is never misplaced.' The car began to slow as he applied more pressure. 'My driving frightens my own mother bad enough but I would never treat her like this and just because this woman snubbed me there at the station does not make excuse for what I am doing to her now. I used to think that frightening someone out of their wits was fun but Eddy and his gun have shown me the other side of this coin and I did not like it. I swear that I will never do the likes of this to anyone ever again—with one exception,' he amended, 'If I can ever get Eddy into the car I make no promises.'

Reece braked hard until he could shift to second gear then more yet to slow for the lone corner on this northwest side of the canyon. Slowing still more as he swung onto the curved approach to the main span of the bridge he shifted to low gear and idled across as though admiring the rocky canyon upstream and the blue-green water flowing underneath. 'Should be fish down there. I haven't wet a fish line since I was ten years old—but I'm going to—first chance.' The smell of smoking brakes chastised him all the way over the bridge but he gambled that there was no actual fire and did not stop to look. 'They will need setting up before I try any more of that though.' He had felt his brake pedal height melting down to half of normal by the time he had regained full control.

The uphill climb was over poorly blasted bedrock for a little ways so Reece continued slowly until the road smoothed where the guard rail ended. More rotten, leaning fence posts and sway back wooden rails but at least these were whitewashed. Near the top, on one of very few wide parts of the nearly two mile crossing, they met another car. Both drivers swerved to their right hand side and passed with room to spare—a good full four inches of it.

The other car was an ancient, tall, single seated affair with a cloth top flapping loosely on four wooden posts. The windshield was folded forward to give the driver a better view of the road but there were no side windows and for that matter, no doors. The driver, dressed in grey cape and driving cap complete with goggles, looked neither right nor left as if meeting a Whiskey Six on this narrow road was an everyday occurrence. His unmuffled engine cautioned, "shush, shush, shush," working on compression. A small tree tied to the back axle by a logging chain was being dragged along as an external component of the

185

braking system—its limbs sweeping along a little load of gravel and raising a good bit of dust.

On flat road at last and back in high gear his mood was much improved. In fact—he felt very good—very free and relaxed and he knew it dated back to his parting with Eddy this morning and the sudden self discovery that he no longer had to be the tough guy. No longer always had to win. He had lost at every turn to Eddy but still had won the girl who rode in the back seat and she was going to bring about huge changes in his life—changes for the better—responsibilities too. He felt ready for all that might mean and knew that until the last two days he hadn't been.

Reece let the car coast as he glanced sideways into the field and then up the tree lined lane to a closed gate of the first farm. The mountain was close and each property along here seemed to have it's own stream tumbling out of a steep walled draw.

"You drive well." Libby's words came reluctantly but with the strength of a truth that had to be admitted.

"Thank you. And you have been a marvellous passenger. Tell me, that 'apparition' we met on the hill—did anyone else see it or was I dreaming?"

"I saw it," Amy allowed. "But I don't believe it."

"There is more than one character lives down here that you wouldn't believe." Libby, feeling now that she had talked too much and too loosely, clamped her mouth shut.

Chapter 20

After a few panicky tugs which only made his foot and leg hurt more, Eddy relaxed and thought it over. Obviously nothing was broken or his efforts so far would have been impossible. Just as obviously, pushing with one foot while pulling the other would get him exactly nowhere unless the horse was lifted or soil was shovelled out from underneath. Neither one was going to happen unless outside help came along and that was a very unlikely prospect. Even Ruff, if he survived whatever developed at the cookhouse, was not apt to come back looking for him.

It seemed the boot was caught under some part of the saddle because he could wiggle it but could not draw it out from under. Each passing second, whatever hard part of the saddle it was that pressed on his foot, seemed to crush the boot ever tighter. Or else the foot was beginning to swell from bruising.

Get out of this now or never!

Once he convinced himself to remain calm it was absurdly easy. Just a matter of relaxing the foot and putting a steady pull on it while squirming as if removing the boot at home and his foot slid free leaving the boot underneath. Once on his feet he pulled out his belt knife to slash the cinch strap reasoning that this was fastest and speed counted. With a few monumental heaves he pulled the saddle free of the dead horse and the boot came with it.

Immediately he sat down and pulled the boot back on—the foot was not swelling after all—grabbed up his rifle and, careful to allow himself no thought of what he was doing, took off running after Ruff. He ran with a limp for a little ways but then, as the foot and ankle gave no indication of letting him down, forgot about it. Blood still oozed from a shallow cut that extended from within his hair down the front edge of his sideburn to his lower jaw but it was not getting into his eye so he forgot that too. The taste of blood in his mouth he would worry about later—loose teeth maybe or a bitten tongue. It hurt all over inside so it could be either one or both.

A horseman first, last and always, Eddy could still run when he had to. Now he ran as if his own life depended on it as well as the lives of three blithely unaware people at the sawmill camp.

Ruff had reached the unfinished portion of the ditch within sight of the lumber piles when Eddy caught up to him. The sounds of the sawmill, added to that of his own fast breathing and the nearness to his victims may all have helped to keep him from hearing footsteps coming up behind.

Eddy slowed and moved as quietly as he knew how—in step with Ruff but longer steps that brought him closer quickly. At the same time he kept an eagle eye on the man ahead for any sign that he was about to stop or to look back. When he got within thirty feet and Ruff was in enough of a clearing that there were no close trees to duck behind for shelter Eddy stopped, planted his feet, worked the action of his gun and took aim.

Entirely happy with his new peace of mind Reece found the road on the south side of the river much too straight and smooth—too tame—to tempt him into any more race car antics so the pace remained almost pleasant.

Curiosity is a terrible affliction. It eats at the mind like battery acid on your best jacket. Baking soda and water applied quickly might stop the acid but sometimes the only cure for curiosity is to ask the question. Libby looked again at the strange brace on Reece's hand and wrist. She had spoken to him once already and the sky hadn't fallen. In fact, he had actually complimented her and there was such a comforting aura of rapport between the back seat passenger and the driver that she began to imagine that a little of it now extended to her as well. Besides—anyone who drives as good as he does can't be all bad.

"What happened to your hand?"

"Ah—."

"He's not used to the Elko wind, Mother, it slammed the car door shut on him yesterday."

"Oh! How terrible. But you're not the first nor likely to be the last, in fact, I heard of one poor fellow who parked back end to the wind and when he opened the door it was ripped right off the car."

"I'll try to remember that."

"I hope nothing is broken?"

"I don't think so. Actually it's feeling so much better already that I may be able to take this off sooner than I had expected." He smiled and nodded slightly to the direction where he thought Eddy's mother Reb might be at this moment.

As they passed around the log pond and wove between and around the various camp buildings to reach the road leading south Libby stared straight ahead hoping that no one recognised her. She found coming back as the ex-wife more painful even than she had expected—especially winding through this camp where the present wife worked. She did steal a glance toward the cookhouse but there was no one in sight.

The lumber yard was barely behind them when Amy cried out, "Stop, Reece, stop! There is Father and something is wrong."

"RUFF!"

The saw tooth edges in Ed's command stopped Ruff almost in mid stride. Stopped him so quickly because the shrill desperation in Eddy's voice snapped right through his own blind determination. After witnessing the fall that Ed and Buck had taken he could not understand how the boy had survived in any condition to catch up on foot.

"You can turn around, Ruff, but drop your gun first and turn slow."

The man turned slowly enough but did not drop his gun.

"Don't make me shoot you, Ed. I really don't want to you know."

"You got that plumb backwards, Ruff, 'cause it's me who has a bead on you."

"But you'll not shoot will you." Ever so slowly Ruff raised his rifle to his shoulder. "Why should you? It's no skin off your nose if I kill those three skunks."

"You just explained it without knowing. That's exactly why I will shoot. There's three of them and only one of you. If I shoot you I have saved three at the loss of one—sounds like a good trade to me."

"But you should've done it while you had the chance because now I will make it four. Ruff now had Eddy in his sights and the two stood like statues each aiming at the other's heart.

"Well, Ruff," Eddy spoke softly as if to the stock of his rifle but for Ruff to overhear, "there is one little detail you have forgotten and because of that the best you can do now is to trade you for me. You ain't never going to make it one step beyond where you stand right now."

"What've I forgotten that'll stop me from pulling the trigger and then going on after the others?"

"You should of remembered. You used this gun of mine yourself and you know about the hair trigger it has."

Ruff was silent for a moment but his aim did not waver.

"What has that got to do with us now?"

"It just means that you are a dead man standing there unless you swing your gun away—and it might be best to put it on the ground for good measure."

There was no answer as the older man thought about that.

"I feel the cool of steel on my trigger finger, Ruff, and you know what that means. It means I have nearly touched it too hard already and the slightest jiggle to me now and you are blown apart. If you shoot and your bullet so much as startles me this gun goes off immediate. If a bee lands on me you are a gonner"

Ruff licked dry lips with an even drier tongue. "What's it to you? You know what they've done to me, they deserve to pay for it."

"Not with their lives, Ruff. This kind of vengeance is not yours to take."

"Why not? They've taken everything from me. Everything I've worked for all these years, gone, stolen. If that so and so from the Water Branch was here I'd shoot him too."

"Sure you would. But you must be able to see that he has not deliberately hurt you—he's just doing his job. It's just for the same reasons as you want to kill those in camp and me too. You want to smash and break things and you are thinking to smash and break lives 'cause that's easiest right now."

"They stole from me."

"They did not! You plumb handed it to them on a silver platter. Man, you have been so dumb that you make me feel smart. I always thought I was the dumbest cowboy in the country till I ran into you but you got me beat by a mile."

Ruff was silent.

"You don't even have to think about it do you? You know what I mean. Everything you have done has left you wide open to be trumped by anybody with half a brain. Now you are so mad that you want to take it out on them when actually it's you yourself who is at fault. You ought to be writing this off as a lesson and moving on from here."

"I'll deal with myself when I'm done with them, Ed."

"No you won't 'cause if you don't smarten up here pretty darn quick you are going to leave your last remains bleeding and quivering on the ground right where you are standing now."

"That's not a big threat. I've nothing left to live for."

"You have too! You have years ahead and experience behind—you can do better. You got Amy to think of too. You want her to find you lying here dead?"

"That's beside the—— . No—. I don't want that."

"And you got me."

"Who are you?"

"Me? I'm that cowboy dumb enough to be your friend. A friend, in case you didn't know it, is one of those dumb critters who will always stand by you no matter what but will try to steer you the right way at the same time."

"I—don't know?"

"Ruff! It's too late for talk! I feel metal parts slipping past each other—PUT DOWN YOUR GUN!"

To die by Eddy's hand was one thing—almost welcome right now—but to die because of a silly mechanical failure was more senseless than anything Ruff could stand to think of. With more haste than he had shown in years he bent to lay his rifle on the ground. As Eddy swung his faulty gun to the side and downward he finally slipped his finger inside the trigger guard and deliberately squeezed off a bullet into the dirt six feet from Ruff. They stared at each other.

"That close, Ruff! That close."

Ruff was pasty white and unable to speak or move. Eddy was as pale as he ever would be. Even his cut had stopped bleeding. But he was able to put his own gun on the ground, walk to Ruff and take him by the elbow.

"Over here, Man, there's a stump about the right height to sit on."

Ruff sat, put elbows on knees and bent forward clutching his head in his big hands, a position it seemed he had been assuming an awful lot recently. He didn't see or hear the McLaughlin slide to a stop a hundred feet away. He didn't see Amy running to him with Reece close behind and Libby coming more slowly from the far side of the car.

"Daddy! What's wrong, Daddy?" Her cry roused her father to look up and he smiled as he saw her running to him over the uneven ground. The sight of the stranger so close behind her did not bother him in the least. Not after hearing all the good things Ed had said about him and seeing now the protective set of his face.

"What's been going on here?" With no answer from Ruff she spoke to Ed, "and what on earth are you doing here?"

"Aw. Your daddy was working on the ditch—you can see it over there and it will come by here where these sticks are. I reckon he has plumb tired himself out in this heat."

"Eddy—what happened to you? You're bleeding—your hat is gone and your clothes are dirty and torn."

"Aw. I fell off my horse. I was just telling your father about it."

"You? You fell off Buck? I don't believe it! You're pale as a ghost and shaking like a leaf!"

"Hey. You better believe. It was me made him fall. I shot from the saddle and Buck got his head in the way."

"Oh, no! You shot your own horse while you were riding him?" For an instant it seemed she would laugh but she scolded him instead. "What an utterly stupid thing to do. It's just too bad you didn't break your neck in the fall. I can't imagine anything so—"

Reece, standing behind her with his hands possessively at her waist had been looking from Ruff to Ed and back again. Now he pulled the girl back half a step. "Hold it, Amy, I think there is more here than meets the eye."

At that moment two things happened.

Ruff looked up to see his ex-wife standing before him and he exclaimed with such profound relief that they all felt it, "Libby! Am I ever glad to see you."

And—while Amy's attention swivelled to her parents, Ed glared at Reece, held a forefinger to his lips then drew it swiftly across his throat. Reece blinked, gave a quick nod and said no more.

Libby was speaking—softly. "Tru, I swear you can't do anything right. Here you sit on a stump with no room beside you for me so I will just have to sit on your lap to hold on to you."

Amy, forgetting her quarrel with Ed over Buck, grinned as she pulled out of Reece's grasp and motioned him back to the car. Reece glanced at Ed—the glance said, 'need any help?'

Ed hesitated, he could use a ride—'two is company, three is—,' then shook his head, 'no.'

As he took his own leave of the group, picking up the hammerless Savage and setting his course back to Buck, he heard parts of two separate conversations—.

"Come on, Reece, the faster we get out of here the better."

"Mumble mumble"

"They can walk down the road. Believe me, they won't miss us."

And—

"I know all about getting a divorce, Tru, you leave her to me."

At the house Amy bounded out of the car but stopped abruptly to look around at her home.

"What's the matter? Second thoughts?"

"Not a chance! Just a breath catchy moment is all. Bring in Mother's suitcase, jacket and handbag please. I need about three minutes to pack. I will cry as we drive."

Libby's suitcase was light and her handbag heavy. While pondering the logic of this, Reece caught sight of the Studebaker as he started to the house.

'That thing will be enlisted to pursue us. But not until tomorrow, I think.'

On a sudden hunch he set the suitcase on the ground and the handbag back on the seat of the car. With no shame at all he opened it wide—changed his mind about rifling through it—reached into his own pocket and peeled fives, tens and a few twenties from a wad and stuffed them where they were sure to be quickly found. Then—looking at the tires on the Studebaker he added more for good measure before closing the bag and taking it along with the jacket and the suitcase to the house.

Five minutes later the McLaughlin, driven to Amy's directions to avoid disturbing her mother and father, rolled it's tall wood spoke wheels southward to the Waldo—Baynes Lake route back to the main Highway.

Eddy wasted no time grieving over his fallen friend Buck for there was nothing could be undone. Buck had been doomed ever since the dream began—Eddy knew that even though he didn't understand why or how he knew. He knew too that since there had been no clear hint in the dream of what was going to happen or when, he could not have prevented Buck's death even by staying home today—events would merely have been delayed somehow. Removing the bridle, he rolled it inside the saddle blanket and tied both snugly to the saddle then swung it over his shoulder. He bent down to pick up his faulty rifle and trudged off in a direction that would take him home by the shortest route.

"Wonder how much of this I tell old Reb?"

"Not much I reckon. I need to do some inventing. Hettie's the only one I can tell it all to and I got to tell her also that Reece didn't mean anything when he stared at her. He's just not used to girls who don't want to be looked at."

Half way up the first hill and down in low gear he lamented. "Once a dumb cowboy, always a dumb cowboy. To think I passed up a chance to ask for a ride home!"

Another thirty steps up the same hill. "Any dumb cowboy worth his salt can pack his saddle all day. How come is this one so heavy?"

Ten more steps. "And so lumpy."

Epilogue

Early next morning before the heat began to build Eddy was at the Spreading Pine horse barns talking to Mike, the crippled old logger who's job was to care for the horses housed there.

"So your Buck horse fell on you. Must'a been some tumble. Hope he didn't get banged up as bad as you look."

"Aw. He's stove up some, Mike."

"Bad?"

"Real bad."

"Oh."

"What I came for was to see if I could borrow a team and that big walking plough for a few minutes. I want to finish off the last little morsel of that ditch of Ruff's and I don't aim to do it with a grubhoe and shovel like he's been doing."

Mike laughed, "don't see why not. There's two good teams here resting up and either one'd be glad of some exercise. Would'a been happy to lend them to Ruff but he never came asking."

"No. He ain't one to think about horses."

"Be sure you drag that plough along with the mouldboard side down or you might bust off a handle."

"Aw. I'll do that, Mike, not to fret."

"Sorry, Ed, I shouldn't a mentioned it but you'd shake your head at how little some of these kids know now days."

"I'll have everything back to you in good shape probably within an hour."

"See you then."

Ed skidded the plough along laying on it's side to the end of the flume where water was running out and spreading back to low ground since there was only a short bit of ditch ready to lead it away. Not much was leaking from the flume for overnight the cracks had sealed up as the boards soaked and swelled. He circled the team in close getting the heavy plough positioned correctly on the second try. Not sure how these skid horses would take to the plough, Ed went around to the front to rub noses and talk with them for a few minutes while keeping thoughts of Buck pushed to the back.

Out on the road Ruff's old Studebaker went by north bound and Eddy watched closely until it was gone from sight. "Reckon old Ruff has already walked up for a can of gas." The back seat window showed the car loaded to the roof with household effects, some piled in loosely and some in cardboard boxes. The pace was slow—obviously taking into account the much patched tires. In the front seat Libby sat so close to Ruff that her half looked empty and he was driving with one arm over her shoulders. Eddy—ever practical minded—wondered about that. "Now. When he comes to a hill how will he shift gears that way? Might be he works the clutch and throttle while she does the shifting—teamwork." He stood there until the dust had settled and the engine noise was gone. "Well Ruff. If you two are headed for new horizons together then I reckon that's about the best notion you have taken up with in some long time."

As he struggled to get the big plough to an upright position and the point turned down for a good start he began to mutter but then thought of the horses he didn't want to demoralise and said silently to himself, 'this here reminds me of why I ain't a farmer.' With the plough ready to go he adjusted the reins to the right length, tied a knot in them and hung the loop over his head on top one shoulder and under the other arm thus leaving both hands free to guide the plough and hold it from flopping over.

"Hup, boys, lets go." Both horses leaned into their collars tightening the tug straps then walked off with the plough as neatly as if it were just another log to skid. "Gee, just a touch, boys, gee," he shifted his shoulders a little to match the command. "That's good." Forty feet along the plough rolled Ed's first stake over with the furrow. The ploughshare was sharp with a downward point welded on, the root knife was also sharp and the mouldboard was long and slowly curved in breaking plough fashion. Even in this dry, hard ground it was heavy enough to cut in and lay over a perfect furrow. "Haw, now—that's good." As the second marker rolled over with the furrow the wise team figured out by themselves that they were following the line of broken off sticks poked into the ground and Ed gave no further order beyond a minor shift of his shoulders until they came to the finished ditch at the road culvert. "Haw sharply here boys, haw." He forced the plough over onto it's side as it came out of the furrow and into the waiting ditch. "Ho." He went around to the front again to rub necks and noses.

"Say, now. With partners like you two, farming might not be so bad."

He didn't even check back along his plowed furrow to see how it looked—it had gone as well as he could expect. In fact, just from walking along behind the plough, he knew he had a perfect water grade ditch. The water would flow or the water would sink, he could do no better.

Back at the barn Ed thanked Mike for his help.

"Say, Ed, if you happen to be in the market I know a guy over in the Valley got a pretty decent saddle pony he might be talked into selling or trading."

"Think I know the one you mean, Mike. Bay gelding, maybe six, seven years old."

"That's the one."

"Thanks for reminding me. I just might wander over there one day." But, to himself, 'not right away though, I'll walk for a while to remind me of Buck and then I'll check with Chuck first—he's got good horses—Buck was the last one of old Mica's and I reckon there's no more like him.'

On his way back to the ditch he detoured to the cookshack to fill the wood box. It was still too early for lunch but Floyd and Corrie, shocked by his battered appearance, fed him anyway while quizzing him about his cuts and bruises. Corrie itched to try her hand as nurse but Eddy assured her that his mother had pronounced it all healable without intervention beyond the cleaning that she had done.

Later, having searched for and found Ruff's shovel, Eddy did a little patch up and fine tuning where his plowing met the older work then watched the water flow. He wandered slowly southward along the ditch flinging out wads of tree needles, moss and other debris that the water had picked up. At the second culvert where it passed under the road again he found it nearly plugged with water borne junk and water spilling over the road until he managed to dig out the jam-up. From there it was clear sailing right to the edge of Ruff's field where the water, with no more ditch to follow, was spreading out into the browning grass. He put the shovel away in Ruff's shed and went to the house.

The last time—. No! Forget about the last time. Other, more pleasant times that he had been here visiting it had been a home. Now it was already just a shell—he could feel it—and a small and shabby one at that. Not as warm in winter or as cool in summer as the one he himself shared with his mother. Bigger but not as solidly built.

Inside he went to every room. Not much was missing other than clothes and bedding. Of course, other than those personal things, there hadn't been much here to begin with anyway. The little bits of furniture in the place were old, decrepit, homemade or all three. Silverware and china were gone but some things of small value remained—not enough space in the car he guessed. The chair he had broken yesterday was carefully laid out to show that all the pieces were still there—an invitation for someone to take it home and glue it back together. At Amy's room he went no farther than the door but he lingered.

"Girls!"

"In the future I will be more careful."

"How was I to know she was playing a high stakes game?"

"And old Ruff thinks there is no serious gambling done around here!"

But he mused on about how this might have unwound if Corrie had not told him there was a pretty girl his own age staying here who needed company. Who else might have stopped Ruff yesterday? Corrie may have saved her own life with that playful advice. It could have become a full scale gun battle with people in camp defending themselves and each other—would for sure have ended with somebody dead or dying.

"Buck would still be alive—— ."

"Some people I like might not be—— ."

"Reckon it weighs out on the good side."

"Nice to know that even a simple cowboy type can be helpful now and then—'specially one who can shoot but has learned when not to."

Enough food had been left behind to make up a half decent evening meal by opening cans though variety was certainly limited. Inside the coffee can Eddy found the envelope with his name on it. Seeing the Rum Runner's initials he more or less knew what he would find inside but he was startled by the amount. "Reckon my patchwork must have held pretty good for him to be so grateful. This should buy me a new set of horse shoes—maybe with a horse nailed on. There can't never be another Buck but a cowboy does need to travel. Even a dumb one does." Hidden behind the coffee Eddy found a bag with three chocolate bars in it. He puzzled over that.

"Why three? Old Ruff ain't been to the store since Reece came except for his gas this morning. It don't fit the numbers. One must of been for me." Touched and pleased he took one and ate it on the spot. The other two he rolled the bag around again and hid them in the darkest corner of the shelf. Of the two gifts, he valued the thoughtful one from Ruff high above the money in the envelope.

While savouring the sweet taste of the candy, he brewed the last of the coffee using the can for a pot and a smaller can for a cup. After eating he went back to the ditch and stood watching the water trickle for a while.

"Well. There she is, Ruff. I said I would help get it here and here she be. But I'm kind of glad you ain't here to see it 'cause it ain't goin' to work. I told you that pipe you let them put in was a mistake. Now here's the proof. That there pipe is too small, Ruff. No matter how much water comes pouring off the mountain in the spring flood or when the other farmers upstream ain't using it all—only so much can squeeze into that little pipe and not one drop more. Then you switch it over at the halfway to a ditch dug over gravelly soil and by the time it gets here—forget it."

"All that work and you could have spit to the wind and got wetter."

"Reckon the Fuller boys' can play 'Rancher' with it as they wish."

"I have seen enough of this place, Ruff. May your luck improve."

At the top of the first hill he turned to look back eastward over the little valley that enclosed Ruff's Prairie—Ruff's Folly. The shadows moved outward before him growing longer before merging as the sun dropped behind Gold Mountain. He watched until only the higher peaks along the eastern wall of this Rocky Mountain Trench still had sunlight on their tops and then he turned away.

"Come on home, Buck, the pasture is good and it's waiting."

As Eddy disappeared into the gloom of the forest he began whistling. It drifted back slow and mournful at first then quicker before fading into the distance. As the last of it came faintly through the trees the tune steadied out and became recognisable as one from The Red River Valley.

An old time love song from the Buffalo Plains.

To be sung by the one left behind.

But not near so cheerfully.

ISBN 1425166369

9 781425 166366